D0869064

It Looked Like ..
But That was Impossible!

Merry glanced over at the tall man who seemed to be giving orders. Like the other carpenters, he also wore jeans, heavy boots, and a coat of dust and sweat which couldn't conceal his clean-cut features and lean, well-muscled frame.

As the three men crossed the yard, the tall man stopped short, his eyes on her. "Hello, Merry. It's been a long time."

Her heart beat painfully. Never in a million years had she expected to see Jess MacDonald back in town. Swallowing, she managed to reply, "Hello, Jess. Home for the summer?"

"Not quite," he answered, brushing at the dust on his pants leg. "I live here now."

TURN, MY BELOVED
Helene Lewis Coffer

Simon & Schuster, Inc., 1230 Avenue of the Americas,
New York, N.Y. 10020

Copyright © 1984 by Helene Lewis Coffer
Cover artwork copyright © 1984 Rudy Nappi

All rights reserved, including the right to reproduce
this book or portions thereof in any form whatsoever.
For information address Simon & Schuster, Inc., 1230
Avenue of the Americas, New York, N.Y. 10020

ISBN: 0-671-45354-8

First printing September, 1984

10 9 8 7 6 5 4 3 2 1

All of the characters in this book are fictitious. Any resem-
blance to actual persons, living or dead, is purely coincidental.

INSPIRATION ROMANCES is a trademark
of Simon & Schuster, Inc.

Printed in the U.S.A.

Until the day break, and the shadows flee away, turn, my beloved, and be thou like a roe or a young hart upon the mountains of Bether.

—*The Song of Solomon 2:17*
The Holy Bible
King James Version

TURN, MY BELOVED

Chapter One

The day after school closed in the city, Meredith Conner began stripping her half of the apartment, carrying load after load of belongings to pack in her small, battered station wagon.

"There's no need to take anything but clothes," her roommate objected. "You'll be back in the fall."

"Not necessarily," Meredith said. "You should start looking for another roommate, Allison."

"Where would I look? Most of the teachers leave town for the summer. Besides, you're paid up for a month, and I hate to go to the bother of breaking in someone. I figure after three months in Prairie Chapel, you'll be *panting* to come back."

Meredith smiled. Prairie Chapel was a thriving midwestern town, living abundantly on wheat and oil. But for Allison, its pioneer name called up visions of mud streets, false-front buildings and a life of unrelenting backwardness.

"In case I *don't* come back," she said amiably, "I will you all the worldly goods I acquired at garage sales: the coffee table, the beanbag chair and that simply exquisite picture."

Allison made a face. "Whatever possessed you to buy that picture?"

"It was cheap. And it covers the crack, remember? You will when you take it down! Anyway, if you aspire to better decor, give it all to the Salvation Army."

"I aspire; I can't afford. Darn you, Merry. I'm going to miss you. What got you on this kick, anyway?"

"Oh . . . I need to get reacquainted with my folks. If I hadn't had such an adventurous roommate, I'd have gone home summers, instead of working my way around the country. . . ."

"It has been fun, hasn't it?" Allison said wistfully. "The summer at Yellowstone was the best."

"Except that I never want to make another bed. I think New York was my favorite. . . . Anyway, this should be a relaxing summer. No job-hunting. My pastor has a job waiting for me."

"A church job in Prairie Chapel. Oh, whoop-de-doo. . . ."

Merry reviewed the conversation as she proceeded along the flat ribbon of road that bisected the sweeping prairie. She hadn't fully answered Allison. She couldn't. She wasn't sure why she suddenly wanted very much to spend a long summer in the town she had visited only briefly at Christmas the past five years.

Perhaps the frustrations of teaching in a jail-like inner-city school had prompted her restlessness. The past two years had been like nothing she'd imagined. Her students were more than her match in street wisdom and worldly sophistication. The goals and values she longed to instill seemed hardly relevant to their world. How could she teach cynical teenagers that good was as real in the world as evil and, in the long run, infinitely more rewarding?

Her kids. Merry yearned over them: the rebellious, the unreachable. Had she made any difference at all?

Squinting against the bright sun, Merry reached for her bag and felt for her dark glasses. After all, there didn't have to be a special reason for wanting to be home. It wasn't necessarily that she needed reassurance, a sense of belonging . . . or to find something lost along the way.

Merry left the westbound freeway for a state road that plunged due south through miles of wheat fields studded with neat farmhouses, widely separated and set in groves of trees to break the prairie winds. Occasionally a rattling bridge spanned a creek swollen by late spring rains.

It was after two before Merry came out of her reverie with the realization that lunch was long past due. She stopped in a small farming town for a sandwich. Two young men, lounging on a bench in front of the fast food emporium, watched her approach with evident appreciation. One said audibly, "Hey, pretty."

Merry, trying not to blush, checked her reflection in the polished window: long blond hair tumbled from the wind, cotton dress wrinkled from riding, slim bare legs ending in shabby leather sandals, face a bit shiny from perspiration . . . They had to be kidding.

The sun hung low in the west when Merry's car

chugged up the long rise and descended into the river valley where Prairie Chapel nestled in a grove of trees planted a hundred years earlier by pioneers. To the southwest, towers of the Great Plains Petroleum Company refinery traced an elaborate fretwork against the sky, with acres of tank farms adjoining, and a great complex of office and research buildings in front.

This route took her past the earliest oilman's mansion, and skirted Country Club Hill, where new homes were springing up like crocuses. The town was growing, and the wooded hills by the river were studded with modern housing developments.

Merry drove briskly across town to a neighborhood of tree-lined streets and large frame houses, mostly white. The design of these homes was gracious, but many showed signs of weathering and general disrepair.

She stopped before a modified Dutch colonial, set well back in a frame of lilac, forsythia and crape myrtle shrubs accented by flowering fruit and redbud trees. Merry jumped out, excited to be home. Then she stopped in shock.

The house was a patchwork palace. New lumber had been nailed along the bottom to a height of two feet. The green roof had yielded to a covering of unstained shingles. Missing were the garage door, rear gate, shutters and portions of the trim.

In the driveway a large and surpassingly ugly truck half concealed a stockpile of lumber, nails, sacks of cement and cans of paint. Merry read the legend on the truck: Hartmann Construction Company. The name was familiar.

A piping voice penetrated her daze. "Merry, Merry!"

A chubby boy came hurtling across the yard and grasped Merry firmly about the knees. This was young Christopher, known as Chipper. He was her elder sister's son, who, it seemed to Merry, had doubled in size since Christmas.

Merry picked up Chipper and received a wet kiss and a grubby hug. Then Chipper flung himself out of her arms and ran up the stairs ahead of her, shouting, "Merry's here!"

They all came tumbling out of the front door: her father, mother, sister, brother-in-law and two nieces. She was hugged, kissed and admired, her trip asked after, her plans inquired into, her thinness disparaged by her mother and envied by her sister—all without the slightest chance of interjecting into the hullabaloo any type of sensible response. Merry didn't try. She laughed and happily absorbed all the affection, waiting for a pause before posing her own question: "What on earth are you doing to the house?"

Everyone tried to answer at once. Finally Mrs. Conner pulled rank, and took the floor.

"We're doing the maintenance we've been needing to do on this house for years," she said. "And oh! we're so disappointed. It was all supposed to be finished before you came, for a surprise. But we had that hailstorm two weeks ago; I wrote you about it. It simply destroyed the roof. We had to stop everything and reshingle before it rained again, or we would have been drowned."

Mr. Conner began enumerating the construction items still in progress.

"Joe Hartmann's our contractor," he said. "Remember Joe?"

"Pillar of the church," her sister, Elizabeth, put in.

"Appropriate for a *building* man, Libby."

Libby acknowledged the pun by giving Merry a poke. It was like old times.

"Do you want to see it now," her father inquired hopefully, "or wait until we unload your car?"

"Unload the car," Mrs. Conner decided. "Otherwise we'll never get it done."

They all fell upon the station wagon and came to the house bearing burdens, like a line of ants. Merry's belongings were soon piled in her old room, which, she was thankful to note, had not been included in the renovation.

Merry's mother now launched a Conner update, with tidings of Merry's brother out West, her grandparents on both sides, and their descendants unto the third and fourth generations.

"Merry," her father interrupted on a plaintive note, "wouldn't you like to see what we're doing, before it gets too dark? I have to see Joe before he leaves."

Merry's mother cautioned them not to be too long; dinner was ready to serve. Mr. Conner took Merry's arm, glad to have her to himself, and escorted her to the backyard.

"This looks like a major project, Dad," she said. "Is the store doing pretty well, then?"

"Holding its own. You don't get rich as a druggist. Now they're telling me I should take out the soda fountain. Most drugstores don't bother with 'em, nowadays. It *isn't* a money-maker, but people like it. It's kind of a gathering place."

"Yes," said Merry. "It was when I was in high school."

"Look. Here's where we're going to pour the patio. That's the only luxury item; the rest is maintenance.

Your mother has wanted a patio for twenty years. Ah, here's Joe. . . ."

Merry remembered the tall, gray-haired man with the keen, weathered face. She gave him her hand and smiled up at him, mentally placing him in various roles at the church.

"Mistress Merry, quite contrary," Joe Hartmann recited, smiling.

"Oh, I remember that!" Merry cried. "You called me that when you taught Sunday school, years ago."

"Do you remember why? You had to sit on one special chair. If some other kid sat on it, you raised Ned."

Merry blushed. It hadn't been a special chair; it had been the chair next to a special boy. . . .

"Came home to an awful mess, didn't you?" the big man went on. "I'm glad you're not raising Ned about that."

"I wouldn't dream of it. Dad tells me you've been working from dawn until dark to get it done."

"So we have, weather permitting." Hartmann waved at the crew of men still busy at the rear corner of the house. "We're about to knock off for the day. The boys are just cleaning up."

Merry glanced over. Her gaze fastened on the tallest of the three men, the one who seemed to be giving orders. He stood well over six feet; he had a well-shaped head topped by a shock of curly hair. As she watched, he shrugged on a blue chambray shirt, buttoning it over his bare chest. He wore jeans and heavy boots. Like the other men, he also wore a coating of dust and sweat, which did not conceal his clean-cut features and lean, well-muscled frame.

He looked like . . . but that was impossible.

As the three came across the yard, Merry's father called out a cheery greeting. The tall young man stopped short. "Good evening, Mr. Conner," he said, but his eyes were on Merry. After a pause, he cleared his throat and added, "Hello, Merry."

Mr. Conner said, "How's it going, Jess?"

Merry's heart beat painfully. Her mouth was dry. Swallowing, she managed a polite, "Hello, Jess. Home for the summer?"

"No, I live here. I guess you're a schoolteacher now."

"And you're well on your way to becoming a lawyer."

"No." His brown eyes left Merry's to gaze into the lengthening shadows. "I gave that up a long time ago. Well. Guess I'll be seeing you around, right?"

Merry echoed faintly, "Right. . . ."

He moved away.

"Why is Jess here?" Merry demanded of her father. "His family moved years ago, when his father was made vice-president."

"Yes. I guess he's still a vice-president. Jess moved back a couple of years ago with his mother and step-father."

"Stepfather?"

"Name's Harry Brown. He's in charge of marketing research. What's the matter? Everything moving too fast for you?"

"Jess's parents were so nice together. Used to be . . . they sponsored the Junior High Fellowship when I was in it. I thought they were wonderful."

"We all thought so. Missed them when they stopped coming to church. There's a saying: If a couple doesn't grow together, they'll grow apart. Makes you wonder."

"But both people have to *want* to grow together," Merry said. "One can't do it alone."

"Hm?" Her father needed glasses only for near vision, so he wore them at half-mast. Now he peered over the top of them in puzzled fashion. "What was that?"

"It was a major philosophical breakthrough," Merry said portentously. Her father gave her a grin. "Anyway, what I can't understand is why Jess would give up his education."

"He's a carpenter; that requires an education," her father said patiently. "There's some vocational course work, I imagine, and a four-year apprenticeship."

"He took shop for fun in high school; he was good at it," Merry remembered. "But I don't think they turn out carpenters at Harvard."

"I believe he left Harvard after a couple of years."

"He'd turned into such a social lion," Merry said, with an edge of bitterness. "I wonder if he flunked out."

"No need to assume that."

Merry looked at her father. If he had heard gossip about it, he wouldn't say so. Dan Conner never repeated anything he didn't know to be a fact.

"Jess is a bright lad; always was," Mr. Conner went on. "Joe tells me he's a better carpenter than many of the older men with years of experience. In fact, he's Joe's right-hand man."

"That's nice," Merry said. "It's just . . . such a surprise. And it's funny none of you ever mentioned his coming back here."

"Why, you asked us *not* to mention him. Quite a passionate declaration, when his name came up one Christmas. You said you never wanted to hear of him again, remember?"

Under his mild blue gaze, Merry felt her color rise. "Goodness, how silly and dramatic," she said. She tried a smile, amused and tolerant. "Of course, that was a long, long time ago, and I was very young. . . ."

After dinner, the Conners pitched in on the dishes, managing this chore with scarcely a break in the conversation. They convened in the living room and kept on talking until the hall clock struck eleven. This brought Libby and her husband, Christopher, to their feet. They collected their sleep-sodden children and bore them to the car, departing in guilty haste.

Merry's long drive was beginning to tell on her. She gave her parents a good-night hug and climbed the stairs. She hung up her best dresses and shook out a nightie— the rest of the unpacking could wait until morning.

Her bath refreshed her. Instead of going right to bed, she paused to enjoy the ambience of her old room. Stripped of posters and photos, it was a little girl's room again: pale blue walls, spindly white furniture, sun-bonnet-pattern quilt, ruffled eyelet curtains and spread. The sight brought a flood of memories.

Merry turned off the lamp and folded back the quilt. Then she pulled a chair up to the open window. The breeze brought the fragrance of lilac. As she sat down and gazed across the darkened garden toward the house next door, she wondered whatever had become of the swing set. . . .

When Merry was six, she was just tall enough to see over the windowsill and be tempted by the gaily painted swing set that peeked over the lilac hedge. She was not allowed to swing, because nobody lived in the house.

Hope stirred when Daddy announced that an oil company family was moving in.

"Do they have a little girl?" Merry wanted to know.

"No, but there's a boy," her father said.

Merry lost interest. There were already too many boys on her street. A boy would throw rocks at her birds' nests. He would swoop down the sidewalk on skates and disrupt her game of jacks. Certainly he would never offer to share his swing set.

Still, the advent of the big van was exciting, and it was interesting to watch the furniture being unloaded. The family car arrived, and Merry would have watched it unload, too, except that she was diverted by a crisis with Miss Whiskers.

Miss Whiskers was the offspring of a registered Schnauzer female who Got Out. The pup's unusual configuration invariably moved adults to humorous speculation. Merry suffered over this, since Miss Whiskers reacted as if she understood every word.

That day the mailman caught sight of her and boomed, "What kind of a dog is that? Looks like a West Texas javelina hog!"

Miss Whiskers retreated. A moment later, she had pushed aside a loose board in the picket fence. She took off up the street with Merry in hot pursuit.

Miss Whiskers dived under a hedge and soon was out of sight. Merry, crying bitterly, started home to get help. She almost bumped into the curly-haired boy who stood in the middle of the sidewalk.

"Why are you crying?" he demanded.

Merry told him.

"Don't worry," said the boy. "My dog will find her."

Merry shook her head distractedly and started to pass by. The boy moved to block her way. Evidently he decided it was time to present his credentials.

"Look," he commanded. "I'm James Scott MacDonald the Third. My grandfather is Jim and my father is Scott, and I am J.S. You can call me Jess."

Merry wasn't interested in calling him anything. "I have to go home," she sobbed.

"This is my dog, Prince," Jess went on determinedly. *"Look* at him."

Merry took her fists out of her eyes and looked at Prince. He was a beautiful collie, smiling a doggie smile and holding up one paw to shake. Merry couldn't resist taking it. But . . .

"I don't think Prince can find Miss Whiskers," said Merry.

"Watch," said Jess. "Go fetch the little dog!" he ordered.

Prince raced up the street, tail a-wag. He returned in minutes, leading Miss Whiskers by the ear, humiliated but unhurt. Merry gathered her up.

"Prince is wonderful," she breathed.

Jess put his hands on his hips and surveyed his handiwork with satisfaction. "Would you like to come swing on my swing set?" he invited.

Merry and Jess walked to school the next day, and from then on were inseparable. In later years there was a season when Merry disapproved more than ever of boys, while Jess went home immediately if Merry's girl friends came to play. But this made no difference to their personal relationship.

In junior high they were competitors, jealously comparing notes on test scores, but doing homework and projects together. They were both leaders in the church youth group and went to church camp, returning with a fund of catchy gospel songs and high ideals. They were in the school glee club and orchestra.

Jess went out for basketball in high school, so Merry watched the practices and they walked home together. They shared marching band, a cappella choir and leads in *Bye Bye Birdie*.

When they were sixteen, Jess could borrow the family car and take Merry on real dates. This led to the first real kiss and the many that came after. . . .

Merry drew back from the window, back from the never-never land of teenage memories. Life would never again be so simple and beautiful, nor love, if she found it, so natural, tender and uncomplicated. To look back was painful.

A sliver of moon peeped over the roof of the house next door. In the slanting light the house looked as silent and deserted as it had the night Jess's family moved to Country Club Hill. Merry rested her arms on the sill, remembering. She had sat at the window then, feeling bereft and wondering if the move would make a difference. It hadn't, at first. . . .

Jess was a member of the country club set, since his father, like every rising Great Plains Petroleum executive, had joined. Proximity strengthened ties. Jess pulled Merry along into the social whirl. Merry was his girl. Where Jess went, Merry went.

The change was gradual. Merry blamed it on Jess's increasing closeness to Steve Wittmer. Steve's father was general manager of the oil company's local operation. His house and grounds dominated the woodsy neighborhood where the MacDonalds' new home had been built.

Mr. Wittmer had correctly assessed Scott MacDonald as a comer, and it was his policy to cultivate comers. Soon the Wittmers and MacDonalds were close friends.

Activities centered on the country club, where Mr. Wittmer was chairman of the board and Mrs. Wittmer president of the Ladies' Golf Association. The club offered a full schedule of weekend pleasures for young and old.

Jess's presence at these affairs seemed to be expected. He always invited Merry. Merry was still a leader in the youth fellowship, which also, of necessity, had its activities on weekends. She had been brought up on the church-comes-first principle. When there was conflict, Merry—not without regret—opted for church. Steve always stepped nimbly into the breach, bringing along a girl for Jess. Merry couldn't object. After all, she had had first refusal.

Still, she minded. Jess and his parents had been faithful in church attendance before they became involved with the Wittmers.

At least Jess was faithful to Merry. He loved her and considered her beautiful and didn't seem to care that his family was getting rich while hers was remaining middle-class.

Their first real quarrel was caused, in Merry's view, entirely by Steve.

The Wittmers had hosted the graduation party, aided by the MacDonalds. Everything was lavish, with banks of flowers, a live rock band and a spread laid on by Mrs. Rosie Jones, the town's leading caterer.

At first Jess had been his usual thoughtful self. He

instantly sensed Merry's distress when she found Sally Jones working in the kitchen; Sally was a senior, too. He persuaded Mrs. Jones to let Sally play the piano for a sing-along. Sally was in her glory, and Merry felt comforted.

The four parents presided over a carefully controlled champagne celebration, then made what Merry decided was a tactical error: they slipped away to the club. Steve announced their departure and led a triumphant procession to the family liquor cabinet.

The party grew noisier and rowdier. The smell of liquor overwhelmed the fragrance of the flowers. Merry felt a headache coming on and stepped outside for a breath of fresh air.

Jess had disappeared while she was dancing with another youth. Now Merry saw him watching Steve and some other boys playing ball on the lawn. They were clearly below their best, laughing immoderately over wild pitches, fumbled catches, pratfalls.

Merry went up to Jess and murmured, "Jess, it's after one."

"I promised the Wittmers I'd stay until they come back."

Merry was troubled. She knew her parents would say she shouldn't stay at an unchaperoned party where young people were drinking to excess.

"Couldn't you take me home and come right back?" she asked.

"In a little while," Jess replied.

Just then a missed ball went through a neighbor's window with a crash.

Merry had had enough. She headed for the house and the phone on the hall table. She started to dial the town taxi. Then she saw Sally and her mother heading toward their battered car. She hung up the phone and, narrowly missing a collision with the fleeing boys, ran to beg a ride. For Merry the party was over.

Jess didn't check on how she was until the next evening. He wasn't apologetic. He was angry.

"It was bad enough to walk out on me," he said bitterly. "You didn't have to call the police! The squad car arrived just as our parents came home. They were terribly embarrassed."

Merry sat very still in the side porch swing. "I didn't call the police," she said levelly.

"Steve saw you phoning."

Merry looked at Jess, wide-eyed.

"I don't mean to question your word, Merry," Jess said more gently. "Do you mind telling me who you were phoning?"

"I was phoning a taxi. I saw Sally and her mother leaving, so I went with them instead. And if that's all you need to know, Jess, I'd like to be excused now."

"Please don't run off." Jess sat beside her in the porch swing, imprisoning her hands. "I'm sorry, but I did want to know. Right after you left, the police came. You'd just used the phone. What would anybody think?"

"Anybody who *could* think would realize the neighbors didn't want any more of their windows broken."

"They said they didn't call."

"*Of course* they didn't. He works for Mr. Wittmer. Silly of me."

"Merry, that's unfair. They knew that Mr. Wittmer would pay for the window, that's all. Anyway, let's forget it. I'll tell everyone it wasn't you."

"Will you indeed. I'm amazed at your priorities. It doesn't even seem to faze you that the party was becoming a drunken brawl, and you wouldn't bring me home. Incidentally, what's your rationale for that, Mr. Inquisitor?''

"I was *going* to take you home as soon as the folks came. The club closes at one; I knew it wouldn't be long. Didn't I say so? Well, maybe not. I had my mind on Steve. As you know, he was feeling no pain. I'm sorry. I blew it. Please, honey—don't be mad anymore.''

Merry's anger melted, leaving her vulnerable. Jess perceived his advantage, gathered her in his arms and kissed her soundly.

"Not here," Merry whispered helplessly.

"Let's drive out to the lake," Jess suggested.

After a while the moon rose to lay a silver sheen on the lake, and a silver spell on the two young people, who felt blissful and invincible. They made plans. They would enroll at the university and marry after graduation. Merry would be the breadwinner while Jess studied for a master's. One day, Jess would have his own business. . . .

Jess and Merry got to keep their dreams for almost a week. When Jess told his parents, he hit a stone wall. The Wittmers had convinced them Jess should go to Harvard to study law.

"It's the only thing they've agreed on lately," Jess said dryly. "Maybe that's why they're so committed to it."

"Isn't it late to apply? Maybe you can't get in."

"I can. Why did I work so hard in school? If my grades and scores were low, even Mr. Wittmer's connections wouldn't get me in."

"We'll just have to live for summers and holidays."

"We won't even have them, Merry. Dad's going to be

promoted and moved East this fall. It's hush-hush, but we're going to spend time up there this summer looking for a place to live.''

Merry was too stunned to cry.

"I'm eighteen," Jess said. His clear brown eyes studied her. "I could refuse, and strike out on my own."

"And risk losing your chance at an education?"

"I'm more concerned about the risk of losing you."

"No risk there, Jess. Not as long as you want me."

Jess reached for her. They kissed and clung to each other until the sinking moon warned them to head for home.

By fall they were more than a thousand miles apart. Jess wasn't allowed to fly to Prairie Chapel for Christmas, but he promised to come home with Steve at the end of school. Instead, Steve went abroad with a group of fellow students.

In late August, Merry, who had worked that summer in her father's drugstore, ran into Steve at the fountain. He visited cheerily and brought out pictures snapped during a campus party at their residence house. The charmer at Jess's side, Steve reported, was a Vassar girl. Her family lived near Jess's in Westport.

"Jess has an eye for good-looking blondes," Steve said, grinning.

When Merry returned to the university that fall, she immersed herself in school. Jess finally wrote, referring vaguely to a "situation too complicated to bother you with" and saying he needed "time to get my life straightened out." Merry read that to her new roommate, Allison.

"Sounds like a cop-out," said Allison.

"I'll give him all the time he needs," Merry said resolutely.

She didn't answer the letter. In the summer, she and Allison worked at Yellowstone. Each summer thereafter they tried a different area. In time Merry stopped wondering what had happened to Jess. . . .

I don't care at all anymore, Merry told the moon. She had sat in the window so long she felt cold and cramped.

She rose. Surely, as tired as she was, she could stop thinking now and go to sleep.

Chapter Two

The tapping began early. Merry, too deeply asleep to be roused, incorporated it into her dream. Someone wanted to come in, and she wanted to open the door. But she couldn't move . . .

Finally she dragged her eyes open and looked at the clock on the nightstand. Almost nine. The tapping, of course, came from the hammers of the men at work outside.

It sounded close. Merry slipped out of bed and eased the window open. She couldn't see anyone below. She leaned out a little farther, too absorbed in this enterprise to notice the car that drew up behind hers at the sidewalk.

"You can't see anything from there; we're around in back," called a voice from below.

Merry turned around too quickly and bumped her

head on the window above her. She looked down. It was Jess.

"You startled me," she complained, rubbing her head and regarding him reproachfully. "And made me bump my head, and besides all that, you're late."

"I'm not late. I've been here since seven. Just went to the hardware store. Out doing the world's work, while some people are lounging at the window in their see-through skivvies."

Merry popped back in like a cuckoo in a clock and dived blushing to the mirror. Her modest gown was completely opaque.

The blush faded, and a dimple appeared. She was a victim of Jess's deadpan teasing, a feature of their relationship in happier days. Jess had delighted in telling her something outrageous, then embellishing it until even the innocent Merry wised up. She was, he said, Miss Gullible, and her pilgrimage through life should be memorialized as *Gullible's Travels*.

Merry picked up her brush and began to stroke her tumbled hair, wondering just how gullible she had been. The dimple disappeared.

Her mother called from the foot of the stairs. "Merry, are you up? Want to have a cup of coffee with Daddy before he goes?"

"Sure."

Merry threw on a robe and slippers and padded downstairs. She hugged her parents, then sat down at the table. There was fresh-squeezed orange juice, and the blueberry muffins were just coming out of the oven. Merry experienced a sense of well-being.

"I'll put on your eggs and bacon," her mother said.

"Juice and muffins—that's plenty."

"Better eat a decent breakfast and put some meat on your bones," her father advised. "You hardly cast a shadow. What's on the agenda for today?"

"I'm going to call Friar Tuck the first thing. If he can check me out today, I'll start work Monday."

"He's expecting you," Mr. Conner assured her, recalling the nickname everyone used for Pastor Tucker.

He finished his coffee, then got up and found a tray and three mugs. He filled the mugs, put some muffins on a plate and started off with the tray.

"Dad always takes some coffee to the workmen," her mother explained.

"You forgot cream," said Merry.

"They all take it black."

"Jess likes cream. He'll take it black, but he'd rather have cream."

"Is that right?" Her father found the pitcher and a spoon, and exited with the tray.

"I guess I should go upstairs and get dressed," Merry said.

"No hurry. Pastor Tucker doesn't go in until ten on Fridays."

Mr. Conner returned. "Jess does like cream," he announced. "Imagine your remembering."

"I'm a veritable mine of useless information," said Merry.

Since Merry was ready early, she decided to walk the eight blocks to the church. As she started out the door, her mother called, "Could you go tell Jess that Joe wants him on the phone?"

Merry went back and gave Jess the message. He walked toward the house with her.

"Guess you've grown up after all," he said, looking

her over. "Yesterday you still looked like a teenager—today, very Miss Conner-ish."

"If that's supposed to be a compliment, I'm underwhelmed," said Merry, patting the shining hair she had caught in a chignon at the back of her head. "I'm trying to look like a Christian education director, and I'll thank you to show a little respect."

"I will, I will! Are you getting a job here?"

"Just for the summer."

"Oh."

"Go on in, Jess. You can use the kitchen phone."

She left him at the back door and walked to the front. As she passed her car, she noticed Jess's pulled up behind it. She paused to admire the newer car, a jaunty sports coupe. Quite a contrast to her battered relic. Merry decided this summer to treat the station wagon to a new coat of paint.

As she walked down tree-shaded streets redolent of flowering shrubs and fruit trees, Merry breathed it all in, wondering why she had stayed away so long. Let those who would disparage her town walk its streets in the month of May.

Pastor John Tucker awaited her. He was a tall man, growing stout with advancing years. He had a rosy, guileless face, twinkly blue eyes and a halo of silvery hair. The effect, especially when he was in his Sunday morning cassock, had earned him his nickname Friar Tuck. He didn't mind.

Merry got a fatherly hug from the pastor, who had known her all her life.

"You ready to go to work?" he inquired, after the amenities had been observed.

"Right away," said Merry.

"Good. As I told you, you're replacing our Mrs. Brigham for the summer while she nurses her mother. She already has everything scheduled. Can you be here tomorrow morning to get organized for Sunday? We have Sunday school during both services. There's a regular teacher for each class, but if someone calls in sick, it's up to you to find a substitute. Then there's attendance figures to compile, offering and a few items we never anticipate until they hit us in the eye."

During the morning Merry was introduced to the secretary, the finance officer and the custodian. After she'd been shown her office, the resource library and the supply cupboard, she was given an overview of the summer schedule for the youth, including all the check-lists for camp.

"It's almost twelve-thirty," Friar Tuck announced with an air of discovery. "Are you sufficiently confused? Take a lunch break. I have an appointment today, but next week we'll have a staff luncheon to welcome you. This afternoon young David—my assistant Pastor —will be in; he's been out making calls. We'll get the two of you together."

Merry walked downtown. She didn't see a soul she knew. Somewhat disconsolately she wandered into the Pioneer Café.

Someone cried, "Merry Conner!"

The glowing girl at the window table was smiling and waving. She was a vision: warm dark eyes, radiant smile, hair falling in burnished waves the color of old gold.

"You've forgotten me," the girl observed, though her smile lost none of its radiance. "I'm Sally Jones."

"Sally!" Merry hurried to squeeze the proffered

hands. "I haven't forgotten you for one minute! I just didn't *recognize* you. You're absolutely smashing, Sally."

"So are you. But then, you always were. And kind. I'm still old Sal, under the war paint. Can you join me?"

"Love to." Merry sat down. "Are you having lunch?"

"Just coffee. I'm being picked up at the corner at one. Go ahead and order, and we'll talk until I have to go."

"I just want a salad. Mother's been feeding me like a Thanksgiving turkey."

Sally signaled the waitress, and Merry gave her order.

"Now tell me all about yourself," Sally commanded.

Merry brought Sally up to date, concluding, "So now I've completed two years running up the down staircase, and I've come home to discover my highest level of incompetence."

Sally bubbled with laughter. "You'll be an old hand in a week or so," she predicted.

"What are *you* doing, Sally?"

"It's a fun job, though it has its drawbacks. You know Hideaway, Incorporated, the company that built one of its vacation spas here?"

"I think I noticed a big new complex near the highway."

"That's it. They have a lounge called the Hideaway. I'm the entertainment. I play the piano, and sing and try to get some audience participation. I'm billed as 'Sally's Sing-along.'"

"Sounds wonderful."

"They pay well, and you know that sort of thing is pure recreation for me. Mother's not enthusiastic about it, though."

"Why not? I wouldn't think that type of lounge would be a rowdy place."

"It isn't. It's just that no kind of lounge appeals to Mother. Because of Dad, you know."

Merry looked at her blankly. "Well no, I guess I *don't* know," she said.

"Dad was an alcoholic," Sally said bluntly. "That's why he died so young. Your father must have known."

"If so, he never mentioned it. You've heard the old saying about not speaking until you ask yourself, 'Is it true? Is it kind? Is it necessary?' Well, Dad is one who actually *practices* that."

As Sally thought that over, her eyes began to twinkle. "Must be maddening sometimes."

"It is," Merry admitted. "Anyway, I want to hear 'Sally's Sing-along.' "

"The new education director of our church disporting herself in a lounge? What'll thinkle peep?"

"Nothing to peep about. As it happens, I don't drink, but I don't carry an ax and a sign. I can order soft drinks, can't I?"

"Certainly—I always do. You could have my old favorite: soda water with a twist of lemon. No calories, no stigma, no taste. But, Merry, I think you should have an escort."

"You sound exactly like my mother."

"I sound like mine, too. Isn't it aggravating how often their hopelessly old-fashioned ideas turn out to be rather practical? If you walk in there alone, all the lonesome traveling men will converge on you. It can be a nuisance."

"Oh."

"It's no problem, though. If you don't have anyone in

mind, I'll just ask Jess to bring you. He rides shotgun for me, so to speak, on Saturday nights.''

"Jess MacDonald?" Merry asked, to make sure.

"Who else? He's living here now. I thought you might have talked to him; he's working on your house.''

"I talked to him this morning. He criticized my get-up.''

"He must have been teasing; you always look gorgeous. He's really a lamb. Why am I telling you? You were friends before I really knew either of you. Jess and I are having lunch today. I'll mention it, if you're sure you really want to come.''

Merry felt trapped. Any objection to this arrangement would be interpreted as a put-down of Sally's job. "Of course I want to come," she said firmly.

"Lovely." Sally clasped her hands with pleasure and, as she did so, noticed her watch. "Ooh. I have to go. Let's have lunch together one day next week.''

"We will, but I can't say when. There's supposed to be a staff luncheon, and they haven't told me what day.''

"I'll call you. It's wonderful to see you, Merry.'' Sally hurried out the door and down the street, walking like a banner in the breeze. Merry remembered the plain, pale Sally of yesteryear and shook her head in wonder. Sally was a late bloomer turned into a full-blown rose.

Merry saw Jess's car pull in toward the corner. Sally had seized the opportunity to tell her, tactfully, that she was dating Jess. She wondered if they were serious.

Sally and Jess . . .

Steve's voice echoed in memory, putting a black period to a long, lonely summer: "Jess has an eye for good-looking blondes. . . .''

Merry put down her fork, not hungry anymore. She

paid her tab and walked back to church through the shady, fragrant streets. This time she scarcely smelled the flowers.

When Merry arrived, Friar Tuck had just returned from his own luncheon. "Perfect timing, Merry," he said. "I want you to meet David before you move on to your other tasks. Is he in?" the minister asked his secretary. "Good. Ask him to come in for a minute, please."

In a few minutes the assistant pastor arrived.

"Miss Conner, this is the Reverend T. David Williams," said Friar Tuck. "Merry, David. Merry's taking over for Mrs. Brigham this summer, you know."

"I'm not only glad but thankful to see you, Miss Conner."

Merry looked up and up. David was even taller than Jess. He had intense blue eyes, fine features and very red hair. He wore a full beard, neatly trimmed; a well-cut suit, and a shirt and tie that appeared to have been randomly chosen, since they enhanced neither the suit nor each other.

"Call me Merry; I've been Miss Conner all year," Merry said, smiling.

"You're a schoolteacher, right? How do you stand it?"

"It's not that bad. I love kids. Of course, it's easier to get along with the ones who are really interested in learning."

"Where do you find any like that?"

"There are quite a few, even where I was teaching in a tough city school," said Merry. "Teaching church kids should be a piece of cake."

"Cake is what they want, all right," groused David. "What they *need* is the strong meat of the Word."

Friar Tuck spoke up. "Now that you've met, David, I'll send Merry back to talk to you about the youth fellowship, if that's convenient. First, though, we should review the summer schedule for the children's choirs."

"Fine," said David. "I'll be in my office working on my sermon."

After David left, Merry found herself the recipient of a very quizzical look from Friar Tuck.

"Well, what do you think?" he asked.

"Is he always so serious?"

"Always."

"Then I think he ought to lighten up."

Friar Tuck chuckled. "I thought you would. Mind you, he's an exceptional young man. Wait until you hear his sermons. For a youngster just out of seminary, he's quite outstanding."

"I hope he isn't so busy being scholarly that he's forgetting what it's like to be a kid."

"From what I know of his background, I'm not sure he had much chance to be a kid. I'm glad you're here. It will be good experience for David to work with someone near his age."

"What am I supposed to do?" Merry asked, worried.

"Just be yourself and enjoy the young people, the way you've always done when you taught or counseled. I'm sure it will have its impact. You have a good thing going for you, working with David."

"What's that?"

"He passionately wants to serve the Lord. So he's really interested in learning."

David had already worked out the division of labor

concerned with running the youth group. He would present the lessons, while Merry could take care of the fellowship.

"What have they been doing?" she asked. "The usual?"

"I don't know what's usual, but they've had a games night, a square dance, various potlucks . . . and Mrs. Brigham periodically orders a movie, harmless enough but relentlessly dopey. Now that it's summer, I suppose picnics and swim parties are inevitable. Don't know why you need to come to church to do that sort of thing."

"There must be some virtue in social gatherings. Jesus went to a wedding."

To Merry's surprise, David smiled at her. "Touché," he said. "Very likely I'll be more tolerant of the socials since you're here to run them. I've had to do it since Mrs. Brigham left, to the dismay of all concerned. Now, if you'll forgive my introducing another unfortunate topic, we should discuss the camp."

"Why is camp an unfortunate topic? If you want to interest kids in spiritual matters, you couldn't find a better place. Didn't you ever have a 'mountaintop experience' at camp?"

"I never went to camp. Anyway, I'm glad you feel positive about it, and I hope Pastor Tucker has advised you that you and I are going to be head counselors."

"Yes, I'm looking forward to it." Merry added with a touch of mischief, "Did Pastor Tucker advise *you* about the funny little tricks the kids play on counselors? The short-sheeting? The cornflakes in your bed? The shaving cream artistry on the mirror?"

"Well!" David began.

It soon became evident that Merry and David disagreed not only on the proper method for dealing with pranks, but on discipline in general. One good debate question led to another; they talked the afternoon away.

"Merry, would you believe it's after five?" David exclaimed. "No doubt you and I will arrive at a *modus operandi* in time, and meanwhile it does appear that we won't be bored. Can I give you a ride home?"

"If it's no trouble . . ."

David had old-fashioned good manners. He opened the car door for her and escorted her to her house.

"Why don't you stay for dinner?" Merry asked impulsively. "There's always plenty."

"I know. Your folks have had me over. Not tonight, thank you. I'm going to grab a bite and get back. Singles meet tonight, and I give the Bible study." He slanted a dry look at her. "Fellowship isn't neglected. We play volleyball."

Jess came around the corner, carrying tools. "Hello, David. Hi, Merry."

"Hello, Jess," David greeted him. "Coming tonight?"

"Yes, I'll be there."

"You could come, too, Merry," David suggested. "You're a single."

"Maybe next time. Tonight I think I'll stay home and chew over all the food for thought you've given me today."

"Then I'll see you Sunday." David surprised her again with the surpassingly sweet smile that changed his whole face. "I'm glad you're here. See you soon, Jess."

Jess lifted a hand. After David drove off, he turned to Merry. "I hear you've already gotten together with Sally."

"Yes, I ran into her today. Hardly recognized her— she's gotten so glamorous."

"She is, isn't she?" Jess seemed to glow with proprietary pride. "Remember how shy she used to be; didn't know how to dress or do her hair? She'd had to make herself over to succeed at what she's doing. Well, you'll see if you catch her act. She says you want to see her at the Hideaway. Is that right?"

"Oh yes, I'd like to go sometime soon."

"Good. Sally'll be awfully pleased. Saturday is the best night; that's tomorrow. Would that be too soon? I'd be happy to take you if you want to go."

A little ball of misery had been forming in Merry's chest. She would have to go and watch Jess watch Sally. That shouldn't matter, and she was furious with herself because it did. "Of course I'd like to go tomorrow," she said firmly.

"Then I'll pick you up at eight."

"I'll be ready," Merry said, remembering to smile.

In the hall, she met her mother, who eyed her critically. "You look beat."

"I am."

"Go lie down. I'll call you when supper's ready."

Where else could one be so pampered? Merry fell on the bed and was instantly asleep. After fifteen minutes she awoke, ready to heap contempt on her earlier vapors. She had thought of Jess but seldom in recent years; she would certainly *not* begin mooning over him now. They would be friends. And David . . . David could be very dogmatic and annoying one minute, then unexpectedly charming the next. She decided she would probably like him, if he turned out to have a sense of humor. Who knows, she might like him a lot.

The next evening Jess arrived punctually at eight. He was wearing well-tailored slacks and shirt and a beautifully cut sports jacket with raw silk. Merry wondered if her sheer summer dress, rose-sprigged and edged with delicate lace, was a little unsophisticated for the occasion.

"You look delicious," said Jess, as if answering her thought.

"You're very elegant yourself. Some jacket!"

"It was a Christmas gift from Mom and Harry." He helped Merry into the car and started off. "Sally's first stint is at nine. Have you driven around to see what's new in town?"

"Haven't had time."

"Then let's go. I'll start by taking you past my place. They're brand-new singles apartments."

"I thought you lived with your mother and stepfather."

"I did while I was an apprentice. Now I can afford my own place. There it is. David lives on the third floor. Sally is in the same complex, in that building on the corner."

How convenient, Merry thought. She said, "Do you like David?"

"Very much."

"Do the kids like him?"

"I don't know, but he's very popular with the young adults."

If David had gotten Jess interested in church again, he had succeeded where Merry had failed. Merry thought she had better not underestimate David. Of course, Jess might be coming for the social part of it . . .

Jess took the Country Club Road and made the circle. There were new homes now, beyond the clubhouse.

"There's where my folks live," Jess said, pointing. "I guess you haven't met my stepfather."

"Until I came home, I didn't even know your parents

weren't together, let alone that you had a stepfather. I expect you went through some tough times, and I'm sorry, Jess."

Jess looked over in surprise. "It's very old news, Merry. Mom and Harry were married two years ago; Dad remarried two years before that. I'd have thought someone would have mentioned it."

"I've only been home briefly at Christmas, it's always really hectic. I suppose people assumed *you* had told me, so there would be no reason to bring it up."

"At the time I didn't tell you or anybody else," Jess said soberly. "I kept hoping my father would decide we had something worth keeping, and come back. Instead, he insisted on a divorce, marrying his young lady as soon as the law allowed. No reason to hide it then; I meant to tell you the next time I saw you. But I never saw you."

"No matter," Merry said hastily. "I'm just sorry, that's all."

"We got used to it in time," Jess said. "Even Mom did, thanks to Harry. Now, there's a princely man. He was a widower, and lonely, so Mom is good for him, too. Harry and I get along very well. He assumes I have the good sense to make my own decisions. My father never extended me that courtesy."

Jess pulled the car off on a promontory.

"I wanted to show you this, Merry. See all the lights in the valley? That was all woods and wheat fields when we were growing up."

"Oh," Merry sighed, "I know people have to live somewhere, but that was the prettiest valley."

"It was," Jess agreed. He was silent for so long that Merry jumped when he spoke. "I wrote you," he said abruptly. "I was trying to tell you, without exactly spelling it out, that our family was having problems. Looking back, it must have seemed pretty ambiguous.''

"It certainly did," said Merry crisply.

"Should have told you straight out," Jess decided. "I'm no good at dissembling; I'd have made a lousy lawyer. You don't remember, do you, what I *did* write?"

"Oh yes, I remember. You said you needed time to straighten out your life."

"Well, I did need time. I was one mixed-up fellow."

Merry felt a prickle; her emotions toward Jess were still sensitive. "I hadn't thought I was taking up so much of your time," she said.

Jess looked at her attentively. "So I succeeded in making you good and mad," he observed.

"You could say that. Of course, I didn't know *you* had any problems. I thought you were living it up at Harvard with house parties and all, while your parents enjoyed the good life at Westport."

"It did seem that way at first. I got my eyes open when I went home that summer. Then things went from bad to worse. Anyway, I meant to come back and see you the first chance I got. I did come, the summer after my sophomore year. Did anyone ever tell you?"

"No. The second summer? I was in Yellowstone."

"So I found out. I was going to surprise you—a dumb thing to do, of course. My surprise backfired."

"Oh, poor Jess!" cried Merry. She had an impulse to reach for his hand, but she stopped herself. "Of course, you could have gotten in touch with me through the Park Service," she said.

"So your folks said, but I had the strongest feeling they thought it was a lost cause," Jess said. "Apparently I was right, and that's why they never told you I came."

"I'm afraid I had told them never to mention your

name, or some such melodramatic nonsense,'' Merry said uncomfortably. "I'm sorry you made the trip for nothing.''

"There's no reason to apologize, Merry. I shouldn't have expected you to go on caring when I had given you so little reason. As for the trip, it wasn't for nothing; it was a turning point.

"I went back to Steve's house, and he took me out on the town; that was our reflex response to adversity, those days. There's a bar at the old Cherokee Strip Hotel, where I meant to get drunk. Sally was playing there, and we hadn't seen each other since high school, but she took one look at me and knew I was headed for trouble. She coaxed me into singing with her, got me to sit on the piano bench, kept me talking. Kept me sober until I got over the notion of getting drunk. I've never wanted to since. Later she sat with us and let me talk until poor Steve went to sleep on the table.''

"What did you talk about?'' Merry asked, very quietly.

"Not about you, princess—you were all ready to be offended, weren't you? What was there to talk about? You'd written me off for gross neglect; I understood that. But there was a lot I'd kept bottled up. I was coming to grips with the fact that I hated the way my life was heading. I'd had two years doing what Dad thought I should, and lost everything I cared about . . . even Dad. All I could see ahead was more of the same.

"That's what I needed to talk about, and over the weekend I dumped it all on Sally. She's a perfect listener—totally absorbed in what you're saying, *caring* about it. . . .''

Merry's hands felt cold; she rubbed them abstractedly while silently taking herself to task. If she was any kind of a Christian, she would rejoice that Sally had been there to share Jess's burden.

She kept her voice steady as she asked, "And what advice did Sally give you?"

"None, really. She couldn't have advised me and was smart enough to know it. She asked the right question. She wondered if there was *anyone* I wholeheartedly admired and trusted, who might advise me. I said without a second thought, 'My old Sunday school teacher, Joe Hartmann.'

"That was my breakthrough. I went to see Joe, and we talked for hours. When I went home, I knew where I was going, and had an idea how to get there."

"Where *were* you going?"

"Back here," Jess said cheerfully. "That was the first goal. It worked out faster than I expected, because of Harry's being transferred here and Joe promising me a job. Otherwise I would have finished my apprenticeship back there. But there's considerable difference in wages when you're a journeyman and I'm learning as much as I can about the construction business. Joe will let me buy in when I can afford it, and he's promised to sell me the business when he retires."

"Well, listen to you," Merry exclaimed. "Not quite twenty-five years old, and the world is your oyster."

"Oh, I don't know," said Jess. "I haven't caught a pearl yet."

"No doubt you will when you're ready to dive in that deep," Merry said briskly. "Jess, we'd better head back this minute, or we're going to miss 'Sally's Sing-along.'"

Chapter Three

Sally had already taken her place behind the piano when Merry and Jess walked in. An overhead light bathed her hair in a golden cloud, and she fairly glowed with warmth and good spirits. Nobody looked anywhere else.

"Hello, Merry and Jess!" she said into the mike. "Some special friends of mine," she explained to the crowd. "Sit right down, both of you, and listen to my new discovery."

A small gray-haired man in a nondescript suit stood at the other mike. Sally rippled through a few bars of "Danny Boy." Her protégé began and immediately gained the enraptured attention of the audience. He was given a nice hand and retired beaming.

Sally swung into another golden oldie, favoring everyone who joined in with her with a delighted smile of recognition. Meanwhile she apparently made a mental note of every entrance, pausing between stanzas to greet the newcomers, often by name.

The big golden light was replaced by a blue spot, and Sally, playing in the dusky shadows, modulated her big husky voice to a soft clear thread of melody, like a solo woodwind. While she sang "Killing Me Softly with His Song," Merry rubbed her arms to smooth away the gooseflesh.

Sally segued into "Feelings." From somewhere in the room a solid but well-modulated four-part harmony arose to augment and ornament the solo line.

At the close of the song the lights went up. Sally gazed attentively around the room, her eyes crinkled.

"Hi, guys," she said. "Thanks for the backup. You sneaked in the back way, didn't you? How was your taping session? When do we get to hear the broadcast?"

Merry followed Sally's glance. The rear tables were filled with men.

"Barbershoppers," Jess said. "They're here in force tonight."

One of the visitors stood up and announced to Sally and her audience the date of their forthcoming broadcast.

"How about a sample?" Sally suggested.

"Thought you'd never ask!"

The spokesman and three others trotted nimbly into the spotlight, immediately deluging the room with full-throated harmony. It soon became evident that the barbershoppers had come to sing and would do so at the slightest provocation. They fielded five different quartet combinations, to say nothing of generous vocal contributions from the group as a whole.

Sally deployed them skillfully, keeping the program varied and spontaneous, using her own solo spots to provide transition or change of mood. She took time to acknowledge newcomers, to play requests and to lure to the piano any potential performer. Sally could spot a solo-quality voice in a roomful of singers. She also showed an unerring instinct for which patron actually *wanted* to perform. She never seemed to have an unwilling guest.

At the end of the successful performance, Sally left the room smiling, to sustained applause, and a program of recorded dance music followed.

"That was wonderful," Merry breathed, turning to Jess. "Is it over already?"

Jess was watching her, enjoying her enthusiasm.

"She's taking a break," he said. "She was on an hour."

"It didn't seem nearly that long. Will she join us?"

"Not with so many in here; she'd be mobbed. She refreshes her makeup, rests, changes clothes. She makes it look easy, but it takes lots of energy and it's hot under the lights."

"I should think so. She never has to use music, does she?"

"Not for pops. She'd use music if she were playing classical works—which she says she does only for her own enjoyment. She used to trade baby-sitting for lessons, but she never had very many."

"She doesn't need lessons to charm a crowd," Merry said. "What a schoolteacher she'd make!"

"She has a sure instinct with people, just as she does with popular music. Sally cares about everyone. I guess it shows."

Jess has it bad, Merry thought. Wonder what he's waiting for . . .

"She'll be on twice more. Are you game to stay?" Jess asked.

"Of course. And I do wish she'd hurry back," said Merry, with perfect truth. If Sally was onstage, Merry could lose herself in the performance and forget Jess was so near and yet so far.

As if in response to Merry's wish, it wasn't long before Sally swept in with her wonderful smile and winning style and performed the now familiar miracle: turning a roomful of strangers into friends.

After her second exit the recorded music took on the slow tempos Jess had always favored.

"Care to dance?" he asked, very much the genial host.

Merry assented without a second thought. It wasn't until she was on the small dance floor, clasped firmly in Jess's arms, that it occurred to her this might not be wise.

It didn't seem strange to dance with Jess after six years. Instead, it was all too poignantly familiar. They stepped together effortlessly, his arms held her in the same way, her head still fit the hollow of his shoulder. He even *smelled* the same: essential Jess, scrubbed and splashed with woodsy after-shave.

Although longing to do exactly the opposite, Merry held herself aloof.

Jess spoke, concerned. "Was I holding you too tight?"

"No, no." Jess was blameless; it would be unfair to let him think otherwise. "I'm really out of practice, and your feet are in jeopardy. You ought to take me back to the table."

"Is that what you really want?"

What she really wanted was a good cry, preferably in his arms. Not trusting herself to speak, she shook her head.

"Course you don't," Jess said, drawing her close. "You're a feather on your feet, just as you always were. Relax. We do have to make contact, Merry, if I'm going to lead. . . ."

They danced beautifully, Merry without volition, suspended between bliss and misery. She loved to dance, especially with Jess. Yet it awakened every emotion she had so carefully buried. Intolerable, to want a man who wanted someone else!

They dimmed the lights, and played "A Time for Us." Merry thought this was the most unfair thing that had ever happened to her.

Mercifully, Sally was soon onstage. She had found an outstanding baritone to highlight a medley from *Show Boat*. At the end the strapping soloist stood in the spotlight to sing "Old Man River." It brought down the house.

Sally stayed around long enough to thank each of her soloists, calling them by name as the spotlight picked them out. She pitched the applause their way and then made a quick exit, beaming.

"Let's go," Jess said. He threw some bills down and took Merry's arm. "We'll meet Sally by the rear door."

Soon Sally burst out the alley door, fresh as a spring morning.

"You darlings!" she exclaimed. "You stayed through the *whole show!*"

"Which was our treat," Merry said sincerely. "You're a terrific performer, and I thoroughly enjoyed watching you."

"I can assure you, she was *glued*," Jess reported. "You were in top form, Sally."

"I should have been; the barbershoppers did all the

work. Are you absolutely *awash* with soda water? I'm dying for coffee, myself.''

"Where do you want to go?" asked Jess.

"Will you come to my place? I made a pie," Sally suggested.

"Are you sure you want us this late?" Merry wondered.

"Sally's always hyper after a show," Jess explained. "Takes her hours to calm down. Lead on, Sally. We'll follow."

Her apartment was small, but neat and new. "What a cute place," Merry said.

"Isn't it great? This is the first time in my life I ever had a bedroom all to myself," Sally said. "Remember, there were six of us. Still three at home. . . .''

While Sally reviewed the status of her sisters and brothers, the smell of freshly brewed coffee drifted through the apartment. Jess apparently knew his way around Sally's kitchen.

Sally remembered the pie and hurried to take it out of the refrigerator. She proceeded to cut it in fourths.

"You're never going to give me a fourth of a pie!" cried Merry.

"No? Jess and I can wolf down half a pie without batting an eye. All right, I'll cut your fourth in half."

"I see you haven't lost the knack," Merry said after her first bite.

"I still go over and help cook. Usually I'm working when Mother caters parties, so I can't help. Cissy takes night classes, so she's out, too. Sam and SueEllen get the detail."

"Well, you certainly had your turn," Merry said.

"Didn't you just do a wedding reception?" Jess reminded Sally.

"That's right. It was on a Sunday evening. I have Sundays and Mondays off."

"What will your mother do when all of you are grown and gone?" Merry wondered.

"I expect she can hire some good help with what it has taken to feed us," Sally said cheerfully. "None of us is interested in catering as a career. Shame on us—we don't want to work that hard."

"Seems to me you worked pretty hard tonight."

"It's different if you *love* it."

"Yes," Merry agreed. "And then, being so *good* at it! Do you ever think about the big time, say, New York or Las Vegas?"

"I'd have to be out of my mind," said Sally practically. "I'm a big shot here. In New York or Vegas I'd be up against people who have as much talent or more than I, plus years of training and discipline. They tell me in Vegas you find Juilliard and Eastman graduates playing in piano bars. I haven't been there, but I expect my untrained voice would sound pretty thin."

"*I've* been there, and I don't think you have anything to blush about," Jess said loyally.

"Jess and I have a handshake agreement; he builds up my ego, and I do the same for him," Sally said, smiling. She stirred her coffee, tasted it and added more cream. Presently she continued dreamily, "I have thought of trying my wings in another area, but one where the competition wouldn't be quite so fierce. Denver, or New Orleans . . ."

"They're still big cities," said Jess with distaste.

"It's all very well to decide on a small town after you've already *been* everywhere," said Sally. "I do think I ought to look around a little before I wake up someday in Prairie Chapel married, with children up to the rafters.''

Jess looked at Sally. ''It doesn't sound so bad to me,'' he said.

Sally caught his look and her eyes softened. ''I didn't say it wouldn't sound fine when you are ready. The truth is, I'm lucky to have this job. It *fits* me, and I might not find one like it anywhere else. But I sometimes wonder if I'm doing all I should be with my life. Don't you understand?''

Jess said warmly, ''Of course I understand.''

Sally remembered to include Merry. ''What do you think, Merry?'' she asked as she freshened Merry's coffee. ''About marriage and children and all?''

Merry looked up. She had sat uncomfortably listening to what was surely a continuing discussion between Sally and Jess on their future. But Sally's reference to children had touched a nerve.

''I have nothing to contribute on the subject of marriage,'' she said crisply. ''But when it comes to children, I get right up on my soapbox. I wish no one would have a child until he or she—I should say, he *and* she—is prepared to put that child high, *high* on their list of priorities.

''I've seen too many kids nobody wants to bother with, and I've seen what the neglect does to them. I get so tired of reading where some so-called authority quotes a mysteriously assembled array of statistics purporting to prove that anyone at all is more qualified to rear children than a pair of dedicated parents. No one is. And teachers and ministers and social workers will never undo the damage caused by what we're seeing now, and that's a regular tidal wave of parental neglect!''

There was a silence as Jess and Sally sat blinking. Merry, as always after expressing a conviction passionately felt, fought off the urge to weep.

"Well said," Jess approved.

"You're right of course," Sally added.

"You two give me an easy victory, just when I'm all psyched up to do battle," Merry complained. "Look, this evening has been fantastic, but I can't keep up with a couple of night owls like you. Why don't you ride along, Sally, while Jess takes me home?"

Two weeks passed before David thought to invite Merry again to the singles Bible study and fellowship. This time Merry accepted with alacrity, eager to see how David interacted with his peers.

David was a continuing puzzle to Merry. She had observed that the older church members, impressed by David's dedication and Bible knowledge, considered him a sort of wunderkind. At the other end of the scale, the small children found him gentle and nonthreatening; they were always glad to gather around him for the children's sermon. But David's relationship with the teenagers—those very youths for whose leadership the interning young minister was primarily responsible— could best be described as an armed truce. Merry found this frustrating, because she sensed that both David and the young people were unhappy about it.

The singles provided an entirely different perspective. Composed largely of professional men and women from the offices and laboratories of Great Plains Petroleum, they were a highly articulate and opinionated group. But David was definitely in charge.

As they worked their way through an in-depth discussion of the Scriptures, Merry's attention was drawn to a burly young blond man who had been introduced to her earlier as a geologist. His appearance and his name, Will De Jong, suggested a Dutch origin, which his southwestern accent belied.

Will's keen insights and formidable vocabulary seemed at odds with his cowboy drawl. Merry listened to him, smiling, until the impact of observing eyes drew her gaze. Turning her head, and facing Jess, who had just joined the group, she kept her smile casual, even as she felt her color rise.

The debate had reached a stalemate and the group petitioned David for a summing up. A prayer ended the session before the group adjourned to the social hall. While two men put up the volleyball net, several concentrated on Merry as a newcomer presumably needing welcome.

"What did you think of our study?" Will asked.

"Interesting. But I don't know if I'll be here long enough to get through the Gospel of John," Merry said, smiling.

"At the rate we're going, none of us will *live* long enough," someone put in.

They all laughed.

"When you go through the gospels with David, you remember what you've read," Will said, apparently in defense of the slow pace. "I grew up in a Christian home, but I was never interested in Bible study until David got me hooked with one of his sermons. They're challenging, don't you think?"

"I don't know. I only hear bits and pieces over the P.A. system as I go from one Sunday school room to another."

"Too bad," Will said.

Merry saw Jess standing at the edge of the group and sent him a smile that invited him to come over.

"I suppose Sally has to go to work too early to come to this," Merry speculated.

"Sally never darkens the door of a church," Jess said.

"Doesn't she believe?"

"She's neutral. Mrs. Jones used to be very devout, Sally tells me, but she became bitter after Mr. Jones died. I suspect it might have something to do with the deal life doled her."

"You're probably right. Still, it seems unlikely that God chose what happened to Mr. Jones."

"Well, that's the problem. Since God is all-knowing and all-powerful, we wish he *would* choose—all good things."

"Would we, though?" asked David, who had overheard. "We'd have Big Brother, not God the Father."

"I must admit I never wanted my *earthly* father to make my choices," Jess agreed.

Will De Jong, armed with a volleyball, claimed their attention.

"Sides!" he cried. "Play ball!"

When the game was over, Merry found the lively Will right beside her.

"We're going out for pie and coffee," he announced. "No need for everyone to take cars. Ride with me, Merry?"

Merry said, "I came with David."

"I have room for four," Will said. "Okay, David?"

Will also offered a ride to a young woman named Sara and, having filled his car to his satisfaction, urged others to hurry.

Jess said, "I think I'll pass, this time," and moved

off. Merry supposed he must ride shotgun for Sally on Fridays, too.

At the café, Merry enjoyed Will's flattering attention. Since the evening at the Hideaway, Sally had shown an alarming tendency to include Merry in her plans with Jess. Merry was sure Sally's intentions were meant to be kind, but she felt like a fifth wheel. She was ready to broaden her horizons.

Meanwhile, David divided his attention impartially among the people eager to claim it. It seemed everyone had an idea to float by David, a point to debate, a challenge to throw down. David was the catalyst, and handled it well. It was such a contrast to his handling of the teenagers!

She thought back to the last two Sunday evenings. David's series had been well researched, fairly and thoughtfully presented. The older teenagers listened quietly—too quietly, Merry thought. They yielded the sullen attention of an overdisciplined class, asking no question, ignoring invitations to discussion. In desperation, David would ask a direct question. The silence following it would be broken by Mike Kenner, a young man who knew all the answers but who kept waiting in the hope of someone else offering to recite.

At the end of the lecture, David, looking strained, would retire to the back, letting Merry get on with the social hour. He acted strictly as an observer, declining refreshments, since he didn't share the teenagers' undeniable preference for junk food.

Except for Mike, none of the young people went near him. Mike, who was confined to a wheelchair, seemed to relate equally well to David and to his peers. Merry thought perhaps the misfortune that had wasted Mike's legs had also given him unusual maturity.

The schism between David and the teenagers was the more striking because Merry found that the teenagers accepted her on sight and soon were seeking her out, trusting her with confidences.

The last Sunday evening she had directed a mild reproach at the group buzzing around her, helping with refreshments.

"Why don't you open your mouths when David asks for discussion?" she had demanded. "There was plenty to ask about. For instance, how would you *know* if someone was feeding you a line, telling you things Christians shouldn't believe at all?"

"The best way would be to check it out with what Jesus says," Mike offered from behind her.

"I might know *you* would answer," Merry said, smiling. "What's the matter with the rest of you?"

"David would look down his nose at anything *I* said." The objection came from pert little Julie Martin, whose views on all subjects were held in high regard by her peers.

"Yeah; for sure." There was a small assenting chorus, with separate solos.

"He thinks we're dumb."

"He doesn't like us."

"He never talks to anyone but Mike. That's because Mike is the only one smart enough for him."

"Horsefeathers!" roared Mike.

The group, apparently assuming Mike had laundered his expletive for church consumption, was inspired to a bout of unrestrained giggling. Merry despaired of any further sensible conversation.

However, she found Mike still in the kitchen after the cleanup committee had finished and gone. She guessed he had outstayed them in the interest of continuing the conversation.

"There's a little cocoa left," she said. "Should we finish it off?"

Mike accepted the cup.

"David talks to me because I'm in a wheelchair," he said bluntly.

"Nonsense!"

"No it isn't. He's not used to kids; it's not easy for him to talk to any of us, but the chair gives him motivation. He's a nice guy, really, and he's going to relate to me if it kills him. He's made the breakthrough; now it's easy so long as it's just the two of us. I like him, and I think he likes me."

"I'm sure he does," Merry said. "But I do wish the rest of the kids had better rapport with David, too. He has a lot to share. I'm not sure it's all his fault. Looks like a two-way street to me."

"It probably is, but David's the adult in the situation." Mike surveyed Merry with dark eyes that were a shade too old for his years. "Trouble is, David hasn't found out that kids are human. Am I giving us too much credit? Anyway—kids are on the *way* to being human."

Merry put down her cup, not trusting herself to say anything. She hopped off her perch on the table and went over and gave Mike a big hug. The boy returned it unselfconsciously, his powerful arms and shoulders suggesting to Merry the big man he might have been.

"Now, don't you worry," Mike cautioned, giving Merry's shoulder a reassuring pat. "David hasn't been here very long. We'll probably all get used to one another. Now that you're here, maybe you can sort of introduce us."

Merry had taken that plaintive statement home with her and had spent a good deal of time dreaming of ways and means to "introduce" David to his teenaged flock, so that she might watch the walls come tumbling down. . . .

"Would you be interested?" Will inquired patiently.

Merry's attention was brought back to the Pioneer Café with the singles group. She was confronted by a question but had no idea what it was all about. She sent up a silent cry: Please, God, get me out of this without hurting Will's feelings.

"Well, I might," she hedged, smiling brightly at Will. "Tell me more."

Will looked puzzled.

"What else do you want to know?" he countered.

Merry's heart sank.

David spoke up. "It's rated PG. Is that what you wanted to know?"

"That certainly helps," Merry said.

David warmed to his subject. "It's a wild adventure, farfetched but amusing if you don't take it too seriously. The plot is intriguing if you're interested in archaeology."

"Oh, I am," said Merry.

"Then would you like to go?" asked Will.

"I do believe I would," said Merry, light-headed with relief. "What night?"

As she and Will agreed on a night the following week, Merry looked over and met David's gaze. His face was bland, but the light in his eyes confirmed her feeling beyond reasonable doubt.

David *did* have a sense of humor.

Chapter Four

Libby came bouncing into Merry's bedroom at eight o'clock Saturday morning—the one day of the week when Merry could be leisurely.

It was, Merry thought resignedly, like old times. Libby had always been a "morning person," as well as an extrovert who wanted company the moment her eyes were open. Merry, who loved to read late, preferred to wake up slowly and brood awhile before facing the world.

"Why are you sitting there all alone?" Libby demanded. "And reading the Bible so early! You really take your job seriously."

"It's not just for the job; it makes the day go better," Merry said. She yawned. "As long as you were coming up, you could have brought me a cup of coffee."

Libby was off like a shot. Her crack-of-dawn energy

made Merry feel lazy, but she admitted to herself it was nice to have coffee in bed before one faced the day.

"Chris and I want to have you over for dinner," Libby announced, setting down the coffee. "We were wondering, how about tonight, and could we include Will De Jong? He and Chris are good buddies, and when Chris found out you were dating Will—"

"My word! We've seen one movie; is that 'dating'?" Merry cried. "This town! My roommate would die laughing!"

"Well, I'm not your roommate, and what I want to know is, do you like Will?"

"I like him just fine, as much as one can tell on such a brief acquaintance."

"Chris says he's a super guy. Incidentally, how are you getting along with David?"

"We disagree on a lot of things, but we usually get along."

"Are you interested in him?"

"Yes and no, with reservations."

"Ha. Such a guarded answer will lead me to all sorts of lively suspicions."

"Almost anything does," Merry sighed.

"Oh yes," Libby went on, "and what about Jess?"

Merry, who had been enjoying the sisterly give-and-take, felt her stomach tighten.

"Well, what about him?" she countered.

"I thought, with him working here every day, you might patch up that old teenage romance."

"Jess and I had a nice talk, and we're friends. He goes with Sally Jones," Merry said evenly.

"Sally goes with a lot of guys," Libby said knowledgeably. "Chris's younger brother wanted to marry her. She shies off as soon as a guy gets serious."

"Well, I guess that's Jess's problem. Libby, I don't mind if you ask Will, but don't make it a big deal. Will seems to be a confident sort of guy. I doubt he needs any help."

Libby laughed. "From what Chris says, sounds like you have him pegged."

Merry sipped her coffee, pleased with herself. She had comfortably sidetracked her sister from the subject of Jess.

Half listening to Libby's chatter, she wondered at her own reticence. Even to her beloved sister, she couldn't reveal those feelings closest to her heart. She had always been a very private person. Growing up, Jess had been her only confidant, and she his. Now, she supposed, he talked to Sally, who was such a wonderful listener.

"I lost you again," said Libby, who was not so easily fooled as her sister supposed.

"You know I only operate on two cylinders before nine in the morning. Let's go down and see what's for breakfast."

"I've eaten, but it smells like Mother's baked something special for you."

"Smells like cinnamon rolls," Merry said, sniffing appreciatively.

Libby joined Merry and ate two cinnamon rolls, begging a panful to take home. She had an appetite that was her mother's delight.

"What is it you and David disagree on?" she asked, not allowing a full mouth to hamper the flow of conversation.

Merry sighed and told her about the problem. "I sit up nights trying to think of ways to get David and those kids together. I'd like to do a sing-along. One thing David does do is sing. The trouble is, nobody plays the piano."

"Don't any of the kids play guitars?"

"Two of them do, but they want a piano for backup. They don't really need it; they just get shy about performing, especially in front of David."

"Why not get Sally? You say she can play anything she hears."

"I don't know that she ever hears church music. Still, it might work. I could sing her the songs once or twice, and she'd have them; they're simple, and she's so quick. I wonder if she'd do it. That's a good idea, Libby."

The phone rang and Merry reached for it.

A faintly aggrieved voice inquired, "Merry? Is my wife there?"

Merry handed Libby the phone.

"Well, you were asleep," Libby said into it. "Why, what's Chipper doing? I told Beth Ann to watch him. Cheer up. Help is on the way. I'm bringing a pan of Mother's cinnamon rolls," she told her husband before hanging up.

"I have to go," she announced, snatching up the rolls. "Chris is up. Merry, I'll call Will and see if he's free, then I'll call you and confirm. Mother, I'm off. Thanks for breakfast."

They heard her car roar off down the street.

"I see women's liberation hasn't penetrated to Prairie Chapel," Merry observed.

"Don't waste your sympathy," her mother said comfortably. "She's just as bad as he is. She's on the phone if he's half an hour late coming home from work."

"How long have they been married? Eleven years?" Merry smiled. Allison would call it smother love and wonder how Libby could *breathe*. Merry and her roommate had had a wonderful time being independent. But .

Merry wondered if she would keep on enjoying it as time marched on. Say, eleven years from now . . .

She brought her thoughts back to the present. Libby'd had a good idea. If Sally could be persuaded to come tomorrow evening, the session would be a breeze.

She waited until eleven, assuming Sally slept late. After a few unsuccessful attempts Merry called Sally's mother. She reached Cissy, who promised to have her sister call if she checked in at home.

Meanwhile Merry finished her letter to Allison, only to find she had missed the mailman. She remembered her old bike was in the garage with two flat tires. A bicycle pump was on the floor nearby, and a few minutes later, a trifle smudged and disheveled but pleased with her handiwork, she hopped on the bike and set off. A ride to the post office would do her good.

As she emerged from the post office, Merry was startled by an imperious blast on a car horn. Glancing around, she noticed a long, low sports car at the curb, looking sleek and predatory, like an attack-trained shark. However, its waving and smiling occupants spoiled its fierce appearance.

Merry stepped off her ancient bike, holding on to its rusting handlebars, and watched three smartly dressed young people tumble out of the car: Sally, Jess and Steve Wittmer.

"Well, Steve," she remarked as cordially as she could manage, "where have you been keeping yourself?"

"On the West Coast, the last couple of years," Steve said. His sharp dark eyes took her in with amusement. "Well, you haven't changed."

Jess made it into a compliment by saying, "Yes, she's still a perfect ten, even with a smudge on her peerless nose."

"Really?" Merry worried, rubbing her nose with the back of her hand. "I was working on my bike."

Jess produced an immaculate handkerchief and, cupping Merry's chin in his palm, gently removed the smudge. "Tell Merry about your new venture, Steve," he prompted.

Steve became expansive. He and some friends had organized a movie production company, and they were currently working to get financing. They had a winning idea, something very innovative. He couldn't tell them more, saying it was top secret.

Merry looked at Jess, now standing by with his hands in his pockets, watching his friend with pride and pleasure. Steve's expensive clothes, the imported car, his air of self-assurance all gave the message: Steve had it made. Merry was conscious of an unreasoning flare of jealousy. Jess deserved the kind of success Steve had—why was he content with so much less?

"This is a command performance; the folks thought it was time for a visit home," Steve told them. "I hope you all will make it bearable."

"We'll do our quiet little best, Steve," Sally promised, laughing. "Merry, have you been trying to call me? My sister traced me to the club to tell me you wanted me."

"You're kidding! I didn't ask her to hunt you down. I'm so embarrassed—especially since I was looking for a favor."

"Your wish is Cissy's command; she's admired you ever since you had the lead in some operetta," Sally said, smiling. "What can I do for you?"

Merry told her, half expecting some cynical comment from Steve. But Steve remained on good behavior, and Sally agreed without reservation.

"Of course I will; it'll be fun," she said. "Though it would be a good idea for you to sing through the songs with me beforehand. I don't have a piano at the apartment, but you could come over to Mother's."

"Why not just meet at the church? I have a key. Would you be free for an hour later this afternoon? I'll go home and change out of these grubby clothes before anybody else has to wash my face for me."

"It was a pleasure," Jess said. "What time are you two getting together? I love gospel music. Can I come along and listen?"

"You can come along and help sing," Merry said. "You know most of the songs, from camp. What about you, Steve?"

"Into a church? It would collapse. I'm going to drop these two off and head home. Merry, no doubt I'll be seeing you at some bash or other. Meantime, don't fall in any grease pits."

The car swooped off. Merry gave the bike's kickstand a good thwack with her heel—and felt it smartly through her thin tennis shoe. All right, Lord, she thought. I'll behave.

At home, Libby called to announce that Will had practically fallen through the telephone accepting her invitation. Merry decided to dress with care before she met Sally and Jess, thus compensating for her grubby appearance earlier. The change had the desired effect when Sally cried, "Aren't you glamorous!"

"And you smell heavenly," Jess added.

"Go ahead. Spoil me. Make me insufferable," Merry encouraged. "Here's the piano. Now you get your just desserts for being so good, Sally. Do you know what Friar Tuck says the reward is for a good job well done?"

"No, what?"

"More work," Merry declaimed sternly.

Sally grinned, running her fingers over the keyboard.

It proved a magic hour. Sally almost instantaneously picked up each tune Merry sang, lifting her own voice in harmony as she played. Jess chimed in with a third part. Merry felt a rush of affection for these two kindred souls. Whatever old emotions she had to bury, she wanted Sally and Jess for friends, always.

When it was time to stop, they did so with reluctance. As Sally closed the piano, Jess asked Merry, "Are you busy tonight?"

Merry said, "Yes, sorry. I have a dinner engagement."

Behind Jess, Merry was surprised to see Sally's mobile face drop in disappointment.

"Next time, ask me a little earlier," Merry added. "Libby just dreamed up her dinner party this morning. I really would like to come and hear Sally again."

"How about next Saturday?" Jess asked promptly.

"It's a date."

"Should I bring Steve? He's anxious to hear Sally, too."

"Sure. Let's round up a crowd," Merry said, resolving to do some inviting herself; it would be comforting to have the attentive Will along.

"What time tomorrow?" Sally wanted to know.

"David's class starts at seven, but you don't need to come until eight, when the social hour begins. Want to come and help sing, Jess?"

"Yes, but I probably shouldn't," Jess said thoughtfully. "It wouldn't be fair to overwhelm the kids with too many adults."

"I suppose you're right, though I'd love having both of you there singing harmony."

"Wasn't it fun?" said Sally and Jess in unison.

Merry thought she had never seen a pair in more perfect accord. She locked the church door behind them and walked with them as far as Jess's car, which was parked directly in front of hers. As he helped Sally in, Merry tooted her horn, waved and swung around them. In the old days, Jess had always kissed Merry after he put her into the car. No doubt he did the same for Sally. Merry thought such a tender gesture would best be accomplished without an audience.

At five minutes before seven on Sunday evening, Sally Jones slipped into the back of the church social hall. She had left off the heavy makeup she usually wore for work, and passed over her dramatic clothes, choosing instead a simple sheer shirtwaist dress in pastel peach, with flat-heeled shoes. Merry didn't pick her out from among the chattering teenagers until Sally dropped into the chair beside her.

"Sally!" she cried. "I didn't see you come in. You didn't have to sit through the lecture."

"I thought it would be a poor example, breezing in here just to perform," Sally murmured. "My goodness. Is that the Reverend?"

Merry followed her gaze to the front of the room, where David was arranging his notes on the lectern. David had abandoned his dark wool suit—what Merry teasingly referred to as his "hair shirt"—in response to the steamy midwestern summer. Now he wore a lightweight leisure suit in off-white, with a blue shirt. The whole effect, with David's commanding height, red hair and keen blue eyes, was impressive.

"He's David, the assistant minister," Merry explained. "We call him by his first name. I'll introduce you afterward."

Mike, as moderator, opened the meeting, and called on Terry Sullins. Terry stood and mumbled under his breath for several minutes; presumably he was praying, but only the Almighty knew for sure.

Terry achieved two audible sounds: an "Amen" and a sigh of relief. As he sat down, Mike thanked him pleasantly and asked Merry to introduce the newcomer at her side.

"This is Sally Jones, a professional pianist who's come to play for our sing-along. Sally will play anything you ask for. Stand up, Sally."

Sally stood with easy grace and sent a warming smile around the room. She let her gaze, and the smile, rest briefly on David, who looked dazzled.

Mike concluded the amenities and turned the meeting over to David. Sally fastened her great dark eyes on David as he stood, and leaned forward expectantly. The quality of her attention must have carried to the lectern, for David automatically addressed his opening remarks to her.

David's subject for the evening was a continuation of his series on the Ten Commandments. "I'm going to concentrate tonight on the Fifth Commandment," he said. "Who can quote it?"

To Merry's surprise, several hands went up. Perhaps Sally's smiling presence had already induced a thaw.

"Go ahead," David encouraged.

They chanted it: "Honor thy Father and thy Mother, that thy days may be long upon the land which the Lord thy God giveth thee."

"Good," said David. "Most of us think of the

commandments as a bunch of rules. Still, God gave us these laws first. He must have thought our relationship to Him and to our earthly parents was especially important. Now, let's think about the commandments as a whole. Why do you suppose God gave them?''

Mike looked around hopefully, and smiled when one of the girls piped up: "To keep us out of trouble."

"Very good. Anything else?"

Mike added, "To teach us how to live."

"Yes. Yes, indeed. To teach us how to live successfully and well. The commandments are for our own benefit. The parent commandment even suggests that in obedience we will live longer. Can you think of a common-sense reason why that should be?''

"People have better mental health if there isn't constant dissension in the home," Mike suggested.

"Still, if you bury resentments and never speak out . . . isn't that supposed to be unhealthy?" Julie argued.

"That's undoubtedly true," David said. "Often, though, you are confronted with a situation you can't really change. All you can change—with God's help—is your attitude. For instance, in my own experience, I couldn't learn how to be a good son, nor do I know what it is to have a close relationship with a parent. My mother died shortly after I was born. My father provided for me, but was seldom with me. To this day, he is almost a stranger to me. I have to look to Scripture to learn what God expects of me in relation to my parents.

"I think most of you are fortunate in having parents you can easily respect and love. Still, probably sometimes you disagree with them. You have found they aren't perfect and some of you may find this shocking. What I'd like to explore this evening is whether or not such circumstances exempt us from the Fifth Commandment. I know I used to think so, when I felt angry and resentful towards my father.''

David looked around the room and singled out Linda Evans, a good reader. "Linda, will you take your Bible and turn to the ninth chapter of Genesis, reading from Verse Twenty to the end of the chapter?''

Merry, locating the passage in her own Bible, went cold. Of course David couldn't possibly know, but what a singularly unfortunate story to read when Sally was a guest! Still, she stared straight ahead as Linda read the familiar story of Noah's drunkenness and the reactions of his three sons: Ham, who reported to his brothers, Shem and Japheth, who walked into Noah's tent backwards to cover their father.

In the discussion that followed, the group concluded that Noah was pretty hard on Ham. Most of the kids thought he had a right to complain about his father's drunkenness.

Merry noticed that Sally was shifting uncomfortably as David sought to explain the passage.

"When I first encountered this story in the Bible, I felt exactly as you do: judgmental towards Noah, and sorry for Ham. However, earlier in Genesis we are told that Noah was 'a just man and perfect in his generations,' and that he walked with God. We have a story here about a good man who made a bad error in judgment. Two of his sons moved to shield him from embarrassment. That was a compassionate act, and it speaks to us today. If we find our parents at fault, we can be angry or scornful or self-righteous. Or we could try to cover their faults with a mantel of love, like Shem and Japheth . . .''

Merry didn't dare look at Sally, but she sensed the

intensity of her listening as David moved on to other Biblical examples of filial loyalty. When he had finished, he asked again for discussion.

Julie spoke up immediately. "Why is your father 'still a stranger' to you?" she wanted to know.

David looked surprised at the personal question. "My father has always kept himself buried in his work, and has left my upbringing to others," he said quietly.

"How can you 'honor' someone you don't even know?" Julie prodded.

"My father is distinguished in the field of medical research," David said with quiet pride. "He makes a very real contribution. When our parents do some of the world's work and do it well, I think that is a reason to honor them."

Julie seemed bent on being precocious. "You can't *love* him, though, can you?"

Merry saw something retreat in David's sensitive face, but he said candidly, "It hasn't always been easy. I used to resent my father a great deal, because I wanted his attention and approval so badly. I pray for him daily; I don't know what that does for him, but it's good for me."

At the end of the meeting, Merry was pleased to hear Mike take the initiative with Sally. "Since it's time to close, I think a hymn would be a good benediction. Could you play one, Miss Jones?" Mike asked.

"How about 'Amazing Grace'? Page forty-nine in the hymnbook," Merry whispered.

"Even *I* know 'Amazing Grace,'" Sally murmured. Merry thought Sally's eyes looked a little red.

After the benediction, Sally stood and in a few well-chosen words dispensed with "Miss Jones" and all other formalities. The piano was moved out so that Sally could see everyone, with the two guitarists deployed on either side and everyone else in a semicircle.

Sally now began to work the magic she used at the Hideaway to include the shy and feature the bold. The group sailed through a large repertoire of popular religious music. For variety, Sally introduced an occasional novelty song. She assigned fragments of one song to a half-dozen extroverts. When the assigned line occurred in the song, each person had to pop up and sing it. The effect was hilarious, moving even the serious David to roars of laughter.

Finally they were "sung out" and ready for refreshments. Merry directed this operation in a glow of happiness. Not only were the kids relating happily to Sally, but there was an animated group gathered around David. Julie was at the center, talking earnestly, wagging a large cookie to emphasize her point.

The teenagers lingered long past the usual closing time. When the last group had finally gone, Merry hugged Sally, saying, "You were almost *too* successful. I thought the kids would never go. Why don't we all go out for a cup of coffee?"

"I'm ready," said David eagerly. "How about the Pioneer?"

"No, come to my place," Sally urged. "I love having company."

In her cozy kitchen, Sally served coffee, then turned her sympathetic dark eyes on David.

"The kids really gave you the third degree tonight," she said. "I thought you gave them nice straight answers."

"That's all you can do," David said.

"I had the feeling that Julie knew she had hit a sore subject," Sally said.

"She had a sure instinct for it, but there's a reason. It turns out Julie and I had somewhat the same problem."

Merry had been considering something she had read. "David, isn't your father Dr. Thaddeus D. Williams, and hasn't he won some rather prestigious awards?"

"That's right." David looked pleased.

"So who looked after you?" Sally wanted to know.

"We had housekeepers when I was little. As soon as possible, I was placed in boarding schools."

"It must have been very lonely for you," Sally said.

"You get used to it when you've never known anything else. I wasn't mistreated, after all."

"Yes, you were," Merry said warmly. "Not intentionally, I'm sure. But every child needs to be loved."

"You have to understand my father. He's very reserved, and I suspect my mother was the only person he ever loved. She died of complications from having me. Dad was an achiever in the field of medicine, yet couldn't do one thing about her death. It was a bitter blow; I don't think he's ever gotten over it."

"What a pity you had to lose your mother," Sally murmured.

"Yes, my life would have been very different if she'd lived," David said. "When she realized she was losing ground, she wrote me a very loving, inspiring letter. I used to study her picture and read that letter until it finally fell to pieces. I still have the pieces in an envelope. She said she hoped I would be a blessing to the world."

"Which probably had a great deal to do with your career choice," Merry guessed.

"Yes, of course it did, and I hope she's pleased," David said simply. "Not that I'm very good at it. I'm afraid I have my father's temperament. I have to work at it to be open with people—it doesn't come naturally. I'm told that my mother was an extrovert, like you, Sally. In her picture she has a big warm smile like yours, just shining with loving kindness."

Sally drew back. Suddenly her eyes were pools of darkness. "You don't know me at all," she said.

David and Merry looked at her in surprise.

"But you are just like that, Sally," Merry protested.

"Not really. By your standards, I'm neither loving nor kind. I'm sure you don't know this, David, but Merry knows: I'm the daughter of the town drunk. My father didn't do anything I could respect; he didn't even work. I didn't honor him at all; my love for him turned to dislike and disgust, and when he died, I wasn't even sorry. I still feel the same. That's not very pretty, is it?"

Merry wanted to weep, looking at Sally's strained white face. The harsh voice and angry judgments were all so uncharacteristic of her happy, glowing friend. She looked anxiously at David.

David spoke softly. "Jesus said nobody ever lived up to the Commandments, yet He was ready to forgive us all. As for your attitude toward your father, I'm sure it's perfectly natural. Still, I expect one of these days you're going to have to give it up."

Sally stared at him. "How do you give up an attitude compounded of dozens of ugly little memories?"

"It can be done. We'll talk about it if you like. But first, stop feeling so guilty." He took Sally's hands and looked into her face. "You're not harming your father; he's beyond your power to help or hurt. The only one you can hurt now is yourself. Anger and resentment make an intolerable burden for anyone to carry around. Believe me, Sally, I know.''

Merry realized she had been greatly underestimating David as a minister—and he was now being presented with an extraordinary opportunity to provide help and comfort.

''I'm going home and let you two talk,'' she said, rising. ''You've both had painful experiences growing up; maybe you can help each other by sharing. Sally, I love you, and I want you to know I think you're wonderful. And thanks for tonight.''

That speech and Merry's good-night hug brought forth the tears Sally had been so resolutely holding back. Merry went off, certain that David, suddenly so wise and tender in his compassion for Sally, would be given the right words to say.

Chapter Five

"We're invited to an open house on Country Club Road," Mrs. Conner announced at the dinner table. "And the strange thing is, it's from someone we don't know. A Mr. and Mrs. Harold G. Brown."

"That's Jess's mother and stepfather," Merry said.

"Now, isn't that a surprise? Caroline MacDonald hasn't invited us to her house since she moved from next door years ago."

"It's really a get-together for Steve Wittmer," explained Merry. "I expect the people up on the hill will be giving a lot of parties this summer while he's home."

"We really don't know that young man," Mrs. Conner said.

"Well, I doubt we'll have to worry about that. Knowing Steve, he won't be around too long."

Mr. Conner spoke up. "If we're going, you'd better practice saying 'Caroline Brown' instead of 'Caroline

MacDonald.' I visit with Harry Brown in the store every week. We've talked to them around town, and I'd have thought you'd be used to them by now.''

"Caroline Brown, Caroline Brown," Mrs. Conner repeated obediently. "You know, I haven't a thing to wear.''

"You look nice in your blue dress," Mr. Conner suggested.

"That's lavender, and anyway, the neckline isn't flattering," she persisted. "I'd like to wear Grandmother's cameo and Mother's lovely rings. I so seldom get a chance to wear my jewelry." Mrs. Conner looked bright-eyed and uncommonly flushed.

Her husband eyed her thoughtfully. "Well, why don't you go buy a new dress? Goodness knows, you don't buy very many.''

"What are *you* going to wear, Merry?" Mrs. Conner wanted to know.

"I haven't thought about it," Merry said. "It's going to be awkward for me, being from five until nine on Sunday, because I have the fellowship meeting from seven until nine. Jess told me that people will be hanging around for an informal get-together afterward, but I hate going that late.''

"Too bad it's on a Sunday.''

"Jess said his mother did that on purpose, to suggest a dignified party. Anyway, Sunday is Sally's only evening off.''

"Sally?''

"Sally Jones. Jess's girl friend.''

"Oh." Merry's mother looked a little downcast. "Well, we could decline, of course.''

"I wouldn't dream of it. Jess and Sally have leaned

over backward being friendly to me; even Steve is civil these days, although he and I have never cared much for each other. I'll go with you; it's just that I'll have to leave no later than six-thirty.''

Merry went upstairs to inspect her wardrobe. Her busy schedule the last few weeks hadn't given her an opportunity to shop. She made a mental note to look for a new dress or two in the next few days. Smiling, she thought how Allison would react to the news that Merry was having trouble juggling her job and social schedule in Prairie Chapel.

The job, at least, was bringing some small joys. Since the breakthrough on the evening of Sally's visit, Merry had noticed the flowering of a relationship between David and the younger members of the church, still fragile and tentative, but promising if carefully nurtured.

Another bonus was Sally's tentative interest in the teachings of the church. She had taken to slipping into the early service, flying out like Cinderella on the first note of the postlude, presumably to resume her interrupted morning sleep.

This was frustrating to David, who especially wanted to welcome and talk to Sally. He could never catch her.

"I'll just have to make a pastoral call," he told Merry.

"Make it in the afternoon," Merry advised. "Sally sleeps mornings and works evenings."

If Merry's professional life was more satisfying, she couldn't say the same for her social schedule. She felt pulled in two directions. Jess and Sally apparently felt that a foursome with Merry and Steve was ideal; Libby and Chris enjoyed planning activities that included Merry and Will.

Merry, not entirely comfortable with either arrangement, attempted to blend the two groups. As she had promised Jess, she gathered up a crowd to attend "Sally's Sing-along." She included Dru Taylor, who had dated Steve in high school and who seemed quite willing to do so again.

The effort was not a conspicuous success, although Merry couldn't put her finger on just what was wrong. Sally gave her usual sparkling performance, and Libby and Chris had them over afterward for a buffet-style supper. Still, it didn't quite click.

Upstairs at Libby's, she stumbled on what might have been the reason. While talking with Sally, she learned that her party had been unintentionally upstaged by David.

"You're unusually quiet tonight, and so is Jess," Merry had complained to Sally.

"I'm sorry. We talked until all hours with David last night. Oh! You haven't heard what happened. After your Bible study, I guess you went somewhere with Will, but some of the others came by the Hideaway with Jess. David heard them talking and decided to come, too. You could have knocked me over with a feather when he walked in."

"Why? He's been trying to catch you at home and having very poor luck doing it. I warned him not to wake you mornings, and I suppose he never reached you in the afternoons."

"It's not that I wasn't glad to see him," Sally said. "Still, I don't think he should come there, because people might misunderstand."

"Nonsense."

"It's not nonsense. Ask your average churchgoer if he

wants a minister who frequents bars, and see what he says.''

''I doubt that David intends to become a habitué. He took advantage of a good opportunity to see how you work. If a minister keeps himself isolated, what good is he to anybody?''

Sally looked cheered. ''Well, that's true. We did have a wonderful talk afterward.''

''Did David enjoy the performance?''

''I think so,'' said Sally with a twinkle. ''It turned into a gospel sing-along.''

''How did that happen?''

''Well, I started it, although not intentionally. I saw David coming in with Jess and the others, and after I caught my breath, I said, 'Hello and welcome, Red— here's a song just for you.' Then I started singing 'Amazing Grace'; you remember he told us it was his favorite. Would you believe, everybody started singing it and didn't stop until they'd gone through four verses. Then somebody wanted another gospel song, and they went on like that until closing time.''

Downstairs, Merry heard Libby calling her name. She and Sally realized they'd been gone too long. They hurried down to join the group.

''Will was looking for you, Merry,'' Libby said on a note of reproach.

Merry spotted Will comfortably seated on the couch, beaming. He had a wonderful disposition, always anxious to try any new experience and enthusiastically ready to share it. He had been playing with a computer video game and could not only clear the screen in one minute and seven seconds, but could also hit the bonus targets. ''Try it,'' he urged Merry.

Merry recoiled in mock horror. ''No, no, get it

away!'' she cried. "It's one of those tricky electronic things Chris keeps around to expose my ignorance.''

Will laughed and looked at Merry appreciatively.

Jess moved past them and took Sally's hand. "You must be ready to collapse,'' he said. "Dru, Steve, do you think we ought to head for home?''

Dru and Steve didn't appear to be ready to leave, but agreed to go with Jess after saying their good-byes. Libby and Chris saw them off, then returned to settle happily in the living room with a fresh pot of coffee.

It all seemed very cozy, sitting there reviewing the evening with Will and her family after the "guests'' had gone. The sense of strain had eased, and Merry felt her nerves quieting. One of these days, she noted with some guilt, she would have to sort out her feelings toward Will. . . .

When the Conners arrived at the Browns' open house, they found that the older guests had, as expected, arrived early. Steve and Jess were on hand, of course, but the rest of the younger set apparently meant to arrive late and stay on. The young men were passing the time as highly accommodating "gofers.'' Merry would have been happy to join them, but Jess's mother had organized a tour of her house in response to the request of several of the women, and she made a point of including Merry.

When the upper level had been inspected, Mrs. Brown turned to Mrs. Wittmer. "Will you guide everybody down to the solarium, Barbara?'' she asked. "I found some old pictures I'd like share with Merry. We'll be right behind you.''

She beckoned Merry back to her bedroom, and produced an old album. "I found this the other day in some boxes that hadn't been unpacked since we moved. Look here. Aren't these adorable?''

The album was full of kiddie pictures: Merry and Jess on the swings, in the Christmas pageant, hunting Easter eggs, picnicking with their astonishingly young-looking parents. . . .

"Oh my," Merry said. "How the years do go by."

"Much too fast," said Caroline Brown wistfully. "Imagine, you a schoolteacher. And Jess . . . I expect you were disappointed in Jess for not finishing his education."

Merry caught herself on the point of stuttering, gained control of her tongue and parroted her father's words: "Jess learned to be a carpenter; that *is* an education."

"Jess could have been a lawyer, or anything he chose," said Caroline fretfully.

"I'm sure he could have. But he seems happy with what he's doing, and that's the important thing."

"Well, he won't always have to work," Jess's mother said with considerable emphasis. "He'll inherit directly from his paternal grandfather."

"That's nice," said Merry. She put the album down and, rising, edged uncomfortably toward the door. "Mrs. Brown, I don't want to keep you from your other guests."

Mrs. Brown tucked the album away and followed Merry. But she went right on talking. "Jess won't even let me mention it; he thinks it's tacky even to talk about getting someone else's money," she said. "But his grandfather has offered to finance him in business right now. Steve really isn't so far ahead as one might think."

"I've always thought Jess was worth two of Steve," Merry said rashly.

It was a tactical error. Caroline now felt encouraged to

pursue the very line of inquiry Merry had hoped to avoid.

"Merry," she said, pausing in the solarium so that the conversation wouldn't be overheard by the group now enjoying a view of the terrace, "I hope you realize that Jess's father and I had nothing against you when we made Jess go to school on the East Coast. We just felt that both of you were too young to be making decisions."

"You were right, I'm sure," Merry said awkwardly. She saw her mother moving past the doorway and sent her a look of desperate appeal, but Mrs. Conners waved and went on by.

"I don't know what happened, and I'm not asking you," Caroline went on relentlessly. "But I know Jess felt terrible, and I've always felt that it was somehow my fault."

"It wasn't anyone's fault—just a series of misunderstandings. Don't give it another thought. It all happened a long time ago, and in any case, we're still the best of friends."

Merry thought she'd come up with a perfect exit line. Caroline circumvented this by taking the younger woman's hands in her own. "Merry, dear," she began earnestly.

Merry prayed for help. In one more minute she was going to have to defend Jess's preference for Sally, and she just couldn't handle that.

An angel appeared in the person of Dru's mother, who wanted to know about the stunning purple velvet flowers that graced the solarium planters.

"Those are gloxinias," said Caroline Brown, a trifle impatiently.

Mrs. Taylor continued to inquire about the care and

feeding of gloxinias. Meanwhile Merry gently extricated herself from Caroline's grasp and fled like a shadow.

In the living room she found Jess and Steve, who had been joined by Sally, Dru and several others.

"This is all very festive and lovely, but I have to go," Merry told them. "Duty calls."

Jess looked at her intently. "I'll help you find your car."

"No need. I couldn't miss that car on a moonless night, let alone in broad daylight. 'Bye, all."

The others called good-byes, and Sally said, "We'll see you later!"

Jess insisted upon walking Merry to her car. "What were you blushing about when you came back from the tour?" he wanted to know. "Did my mother say something outrageous?"

"Of course not. When I left her, your mother was discussing the gloxinias. Jess, I don't think I'll be able to come back later."

"Why not?"

"By the time I help the kids serve refreshments, then clean up, it's likely to be awfully late."

"But I'm counting on you to bring David," said Jess.

"Oh! You asked David?"

"Certainly I asked David. Don't you think a minister likes to be asked now and then to a strictly social occasion, where his services *aren't* required?"

"Of course. I think it's very thoughtful of you. However—David has a car."

"I didn't think he would come that late alone. So I took the liberty of saying you'd be coming back, and that you'd be glad to bring him."

"All right. For David's sake, I'll come back as soon as we can get away, and I'll have David in tow."

"I really do appreciate it, Merry. And I expect you're right in not telling me what my mother said to you . . . no matter how outrageous it was."

Merry felt the telltale flush stain her cheeks again. Her temper rose like hot mercury. "Nobody likes a smart nose," she snapped. "Especially a manipulative smart nose."

When Jess laughed that way, clear from the bottom of his toes, it was impossible for Merry to resist laughing with him.

"You still have that funny little dimple way up on your cheek," Jess observed. He opened her car door and smiled down at her as she settled under the wheel. When she smiled back, he leaned down and dropped a light kiss on her dimpled cheek, then another on her lips.

"That's for old times' sake," he said.

Merry drove off quickly, before the storm building behind her eyes could break. Then for a few moments she drove perilously, on the curving hill road, blinded by tears.

Tears, for old times' sake.

At seven-fifteen in the morning, Steve Wittmer perched at the counter of Jess MacDonald's small breakfast bar, nursing a cup of coffee and smoking a cigarette while Jess presided efficiently over a panful of scrambled eggs. Jess was whistling cheerfully, waving his spatula like a conductor's baton.

Steve helped himself to a paper towel and mopped his sweaty brow. The two had been up until two that morning and had met at six for a fast game of racquetball. Now Jess proposed to serve breakfast before launching his own full day of physical work.

"I have to admit you're in better shape than I am, buddy," Steve said.

"You exercise your brains instead of your back," Jess said, smiling. "All that'll get you is rich and famous."

"And fat and short of breath," Steve finished. "Don't tell me smoking cuts my wind. I know."

"I wasn't going to," said Jess tranquilly.

"Sorry. My mother tells me every hour on the hour."

"She's saying she loves you. That's a quote from Friar Tuck. I try to remember it when Mom tells me something I don't want to hear."

"What could Miz Caroline tell you?" Steve unconsciously used the name the MacDonalds' housekeeper had called Jess's mother. "You don't have any bad habits."

"I have never run my personal life to suit 'Miz Caroline,'" Jess said dryly.

He set before Steve a king-size plateful of fluffy eggs, crisply fried bacon and buttered whole wheat toast.

Steve opened his eyes wide. "Is this my plate, or, more logically, is it intended for the two of us and a couple of starving animals?"

"It's your plate, and you clean it, hear?"

"On the Coast I forget to eat for days at a time. Here I report for meals to keep from antagonizing my mother. What are you grinning about?"

"The movie mogul who's afraid to antagonize his five-foot-nothing mother. Not that I would do anything so rash myself."

"My five-foot-nothing mother is instrumental to the financial health of my business. Make no mistake," Steve said warmly. "One day I expect to reward my parents significantly for any small investment they've made in me. Meanwhile, one does not quarrel with one's banker.''

Steve finished breakfast and leaned back for a luxurious yawn. "I could go to sleep right here.''

"Why not? The couch in the den is comfortable. I'll come back at twelve, and we can have lunch together.''

"I might take you up on that," Steve said. "But I should call my partners first.''

"Help yourself.''

Jess showered, dressed and went to work in a happy frame of mind. Steve sank down on the couch and slept for three hours. At eleven he awoke and went into Jess's bedroom to phone.

A blond young woman, photographed in living color to catch her special glow, smiled at him from the silver-framed portrait on the nightstand.

"Oh yes, you're a beauty," Steve told the portrait, with the detachment of a connoisseur. "Wonder what the problem is. Is he dragging his feet, or are you? He should have married that heiress. She was crazy about him—probably still is. It'd serve you right if I invited her down.''

He sat down and placed his call. He was just hanging up the phone when Jess came in.

"Steve?" Jess looked into the bedroom and saw his friend sitting on the side of the bed. "What's the matter, buddy? Bad news?''

"Oh . . . things never go as fast as you think they should," Steve said vaguely. "Guess I ought to go home.''

"It's lunchtime. Aren't you hungry?''

"Not really. Tell you what, I could use a drink.''

"I'm not dressed for the club. There's Clancy's Bar and Grill downtown."

"Sounds fine."

Steve had a scotch on the rocks while Jess devoured a ham on rye and a glass of milk.

Jess turned to his friend. "Well, Steve, do you want to talk about your business, or would you rather forget it?"

"I'd rather forget it." Steve moodily sipped his drink. Plainly he wasn't forgetting it for a minute.

"The problem is," he said presently, "Corcoran is supposed to raise the money. He has all the contacts. This one outfit Corky's been talking to is supposed to be coming in for five megabucks. Don't know what they're waiting for."

"Five megabucks," Jess repeated. *"Five million dollars?"*

"We have to have that much committed to start production."

"Have you considered going public?" Jess asked.

"We've talked about it. But the market is lousy, and Corky doesn't think we could raise that much."

Jess rubbed his forehead. "Corky . . . that's John Corcoran, isn't it? And your other partner is Ted Flannery? Their families are supposed to have millions in tax-free bonds."

"They do," Steve said. "However, you'll find that rich people are not fond of risking their own money. Right now, we need a hundred and fifty thousand in the bank to keep operating. Corky proposes we each contribute fifty thousand. I'm always supposed to keep up with the two of them, although it's *my* idea Corky is selling."

"What's Flannery's job?"

"He's a good publicity and public relations person. I

hate to admit it, but he's wittier than I am. Remember, he used to keep us in stitches. We work well together, and he has a lot of important contacts. But I'm the ideas man, make no mistake.''

"I believe you. How are you protecting yourself? Are you keeping the copyrights in your name?''

Steve looked troubled. "I've left the business end pretty much up to Corky,'' he admitted. "I think the company owns the copyrights—if he bothered to get any.''

"Doesn't your dad play golf with Fritz Niederhoff? He used to be head counsel for the company before he retired.''

"Good thought. I'll join them next time they play. Dad asked me last week, but I didn't have the sense to do it.''

"Another thing,'' Jess said. "With two fortunes behind you, wouldn't the bank give you a line of credit?''

"You'd think so, but Corky and Flan believe in parity. Corky says, ''Haven't you got ten friends who'll buy a piece of you for five thou? That's how *I'm* going to do it.' ''

"Maybe that's not a bad idea.''

"I don't have millionaire friends. Middle-brow mid-westerners aren't about to take the plunge for a new movie idea.''

"How do you know if you haven't presented it? I think your ideas sound good. Want to sell me a share?''

"You're saving to buy Joe's business.''

"True. But I won't have that opportunity until Joe retires. By that time I figure you'll have turned my five thousand into a small fortune.''

"Jess, do you have five thousand?''

"That's about what I do have."

"Well, I'm going to talk to some people I know who are reasonably well off. If it doesn't sound like a good risk to them, it isn't a good risk for you, and I won't offer it, Jess. Meanwhile, I'll try to maneuver my mother into persuading Dad to co-sign a loan."

As Jess and Steve walked to their cars, they passed the Pioneer Café, where David was lunching with Merry. David waved, but they were too absorbed in their conversation to notice.

"There go Jess and Steve," David observed.

"I saw them."

"Charming, to see a friendship like theirs."

"Do you think so?" Merry responded neutrally. Then she looked up to search David's face. "You're baiting me, aren't you?"

"I guess I am, shame on me. I've noticed there's no love lost between you and Steve."

"Does it show that much? The truth is, I'm being unreasonable. I think Jess is the nicer person, but that's no reason to resent the fact that Steve is more successful."

"Do you think he is?"

Merry blinked. "It seems obvious."

"Not to me," said David. "I suppose it depends on what criteria you use, but Jess's life-style looks good to me. He's doing what he wants to do, moving ahead professionally while leaving time and space for growth in other areas."

Merry's heart swelled with pride. "Tell me what you mean," she urged David.

"Don't you know? Jess and Joe do a lot of work in rehabilitation. They're both very quiet about it, but I'm sure they wouldn't mind my telling you."

"What sort of rehabilitation?" Merry prodded.

"They work with young men who have been in reform school or jail, or who are trying to avoid it. They make a good team."

"That's wonderful," Merry said. "It's just like Jess to use his energy helping people, while Steve cares only about getting ahead in the world."

"Jess will get ahead, never fear," David predicted. "You like him a lot, don't you?"

"Jess?" Merry hastily marshaled her defenses. "Of course I do. We've been friends since the first grade."

"Just friends?"

"We both have other interests," said Merry with her most charming smile.

"Forgive me—I'm being inexcusably nosey," David said. "I've developed an intense curiosity concerning romantic relationships because, for the first time ever, I'm attracted to someone."

"If you want to tell me, I'll be glad to listen," said Merry.

David lowered his voice. "Well, it's Sally, of course," he said with an air of released tension. "Hadn't you guessed?"

"In my innocence, I supposed your interest was entirely spiritual," said Merry with a twinkle.

"It's that, too," said David earnestly. "Merry, Sally is on her way to becoming a radiant Christian, with all the sweetness and openness you hope such a commitment will bring. Combined with all the lovely qualities she already has, it makes her irresistible."

"I see," Merry breathed. *Everybody's* in love with Sally, she thought. First Jess, now David.

"How simple and uncomplicated it must be to fall in love when you're not a minister." David sighed.

"What in the world has that got to do with it?"

"Everything. Sally keeps me at arm's length. She won't be seen with me in public. Just because she works in a bar, she thinks she'll hurt my image."

Merry wondered. Was Sally really worrying about David's image, or was she sparing him, not wanting to tell him she preferred Jess?

David studied her face. "Do you think it's so hopeless?" he inquired bluntly.

"I don't know," Merry said. "It's true that Sally is inordinately sensitive, on account of her father's trouble."

"Entertainers have to go where the work is," David said. "But for very selfish reasons, I wish she'd find another job."

"Where else could she be paid for doing what she loves to do?"

"I don't know," said David. "I wish she played the organ."

Chapter Six

Merry arrived at the church parking lot in the lightening gray of a midwestern predawn. David was already there, awaiting the junior high–age campers and their sponsors.

Dropping her gear near the bus, Merry went to sit with David on the church steps. He was counting the names listed on his clipboard.

"Seven days with forty-seven adolescents," he sighed. "This ought to put some stars in my crown."

"More like a hundred and forty-seven," Merry corrected. "Other churches send campers, remember?"

"Must I face reality so early in the morning?"

"Cheer up. It'll be easy. Remember, each group has its own set of sponsors. The camp has a full-time professional staff, plus college counselors. There shouldn't be any trouble."

"*Our* campers, at least, are all under contract."

"Really? We always managed *without* a contract."

"You weren't here last year. The kids built a big bonfire out in the timber. Friar Tuck told me the Forest Service almost shut us down. This year the fire danger is even worse."

"I didn't say we shouldn't *watch* them like hawks, and do whatever is necessary if they're unmanageable. I just hate to be committed to a certain course of action."

"You aren't committed; just empowered," David said. He brought out a copy of the contract he had introduced, and read aloud: " 'A camper who refuses to conform to the above rules and regulations may be sent home at his parents' expense. It says *'may,'* Merry, not *'will.'* "

"All the same, it sounds pretty grim for a church camp."

"Nonsense. Even our easygoing pastor agreed it was a good idea. I don't know how you ever survived in a ghetto school situation when you're so lax on discipline."

"I wasn't. But the kids I taught needed love and attention more than they needed discipline."

Two cars and a van swung in sequence into the parking lot. Merry and David stopped arguing and closed ranks.

In half an hour the bus was loaded with youngsters, the overflow being accommodated in the van driven by the sponsors, Ted and Sandy Parker. Merry and David rode on the bus.

Merry chose seats toward the front. "The farther back, the noisier," she warned David.

They had hardly left the parking lot before the truth of her pronouncement became evident. From the rear of the bus rose a spirited rendition of "Ninety-nine Bottles of

Beer on the Wall," which was to continue across two counties.

"That's about the worst singing I've ever heard," David muttered. "Who's the kid with the bazoo voice?"

"That's Miles Ross," Merry murmured. "He and his brother Alec are usually in the middle of anything aggravating. Sandy says their father took off and left them and their mother without even a word. They have a lot of hostility to get rid of."

"No doubt you would disapprove, then, of my putting a stop to that racket."

"Well . . . I save my guns for the big ones."

Later, while walking up the aisle to stretch her legs, Merry spotted a young man hanging half out of his open window. She reached over, grasped him by the belt and sat him down hard. Then she delivered a brief, blistering lecture. She returned to her seat to find David grinning.

"So that's a 'big one,' " he said.

"You bet," Merry confirmed.

The ninety-nine bottles came down to one and started back up again before the chanters gave it up for lunch. David, who had been made perfectly miserable, was overjoyed to leave the bus for the relative quiet of a hot, dusty little park.

The bus labored up the mountain, pulling into camp in time for supper at the mess hall. Afterward the kids were assigned to cabins, each housing a dozen campers and at least one adult.

After unpacking, the campers reported back for a program arranged by the lively young college counselors, which ended with simple devotions at the campfire. Mercifully, everyone was too tired for shenanigans. In her cabin, Merry did a bed check. Across the camp,

David counted his sheep, commended them to the care of the Good Shepherd and fell instantly asleep.

The next day the campers quickly fell into the routine devised by the professional staff. For this age group it was highly structured, designed to keep even the most mischievous too busy for troublemaking. The college counselors had taken over, that first afternoon, to give the education counselors a chance to coordinate the curriculum.

The game for the day was fox and hounds. Two counselors acted as 'foxes' for each of the several groups into which the kids had been divided, each designated as 'hounds.' The foxes left ten minutes in advance of the hounds and were obliged to leave tracks, which their pursuers would follow over a circuitous route leading through the outer reaches of the campgrounds, then back to the mess hall.

Merry and David emerged from their session to find worry mounting among the college counselors. All groups but one were back at the mess hall. The missing group's foxes had gone back to retrace the entire route—an easy task, since their colorful "signs" were still intact. But they returned without the missing campers.

Camp O'Clouds unlimbered its big guns. The Reverend Paul Masterson, who supervised the camp, hit the trail with his woods-wise assistant, known as Scout. They would be looking for real signs: footprints, bent twigs, gum wrappers.

Though the rest of the staff moved uneasily back into the day's routine, Merry, David, Sandy and Ted found time to confer.

"How many of those hounds are ours?" David wanted to know.

"Six out of the ten," said Ted. Sandy enumerated them.

"Did you say Miles and Alex Ross?" David asked sharply.

"Yes, and Wilbur Mayberry, who follows Miles's lead," Sandy added. "It's my guess that Miles is calling the shots."

"Would he lead them astray on purpose?"

"I wouldn't put it past him."

It was almost dark when the phone rang urgently in the camp office. Mrs. Masterson answered it on the first ring. "Hogan's! That's seven miles away!" she cried.

"The kids are waiting at the mouth of Colman Canyon with Scout," her husband explained. "I had to slog a couple of extra miles to find a phone. Scout and I caught up with them in Shotgun Gulch. There's so much cover there, you'd never see them from above."

"And there's so much poison ivy there, they couldn't have avoided it," said Maggie Masterson grimly. "Well, I'm off in the pickup."

The bedraggled crew arrived shortly and were sent to shower in strong soap and divest themselves of ivy-laden clothing.

"Will that do any good?" David wondered.

"Well, it makes *us* feel better," Merry said. "At least it may wash off some of the allergens. My guess is that within a week half those kids will have a flaming good case of poison ivy."

The wayward and exhausted campers were then brought to the mess hall, where everyone else had finished eating. Merry thought Miles and his cohorts looked uncommonly pleased with themselves.

"If that was on purpose, what was it *for?*" David asked.

"For attention," Sandy guessed. "Just think: from three until almost seven, no one thought of anything else."

"That's getting it the hard way," Merry commented.

"Oh, I don't know. Miles is husky, and do you know the little monkey told me he's immune to poison ivy?"

"There's nothing we can do, since we can't prove he masterminded this," David decided. "But we'd better keep that gang under surveillance."

"Amen," said the others.

The next day was Sunday, and Miles, Alec and Wilbur were as good as gold all morning. After lunch, however, they disappeared.

They were missed instantly. Scout came on the double and deployed his troops. This time it didn't take long.

Miles had taken the precaution to hide his cache behind the next hill. But he hadn't given any thought to the rocky promontory that gave the searchers a view of that very area.

From the promontory a series of small pops could be heard, and then puffs of gray smoke rose from below. Scout and his teams converged and deprived the three of an astonishingly hefty supply of smuggled fireworks.

"They're going home tomorrow," David announced a short time later. "Don't try to change my mind, Merry. Those three could have burned the whole mountain, and us with it."

"I don't disagree. I just wondered *how*. Poor Sharon Ross barely gets by. Will she have to take a day off to get them?"

"*Jess* is taking a day off, and it's all arranged. He's starting today and will be here late this evening. After breakfast tomorrow, he'll take those scourges home. Jess said the trip would give him a chance to get acquainted with them. He's going to try to work with them.''

Merry's spirits soared. Something good might come out of this, after all, for Miles and his mischievous followers. Personally, she felt a small glow of anticipation. Camp had suffused her with memories. The very air, crisp and fragrant of pine, evoked a time when she and Jess had been at one with each other and the beauty around them. Perhaps being here would make Jess remember.

But Merry's soaring spirits fell when Jess arrived with Sally. The counselors, having settled their charges into bed for the night, were waiting with a welcoming fire in the lodge and refreshments ready to serve. David was obviously delighted with the unexpected appearance of Sally and talked nonstop into her sympathetic ear. Obviously he thought Sally had come to see him. Merry, of course, knew better.

Jess sat down by Merry and tried to make conversation. Merry couldn't seem to push a sensible sentence past the big lump of disappointment and jealousy that weighted her chest.

At breakfast, Merry was surrounded by her charges. Jess and Sally ate with Miles, Alex and Wilbur. Merry, watching, noticed that Jess had already broken through Miles's sullen silence and Miles was animatedly talking to Jess.

During a restless night Merry had gotten a grip on herself. She wished them a safe trip home, then resolutely moved off with her campers.

The week wound down with a Fourth of July celebration, since the campers would be traveling on the actual holiday.

Closing ceremonies that evening were more serious

and brought small miracles. Rivalries were forgotten, cliques at least temporarily disbanded, and none of those on the mountain felt themselves strangers. Youngsters shared their visions; humbled adults were still. Long after the embers of that final fire had darkened and cooled, Merry lay awake remembering its special glow. For her it had a core of wistfulness, both for herself and for the three who had left unwarmed.

They departed in the chilly dawn, in a hail of tears and pledges of undying friendship. For some miles she and David rode in unprecedented quiet until David broke the silence. "Still mourning over Miles?"

"Yes. Oh, I know we had to do it. He was getting back at everyone, and glorying in it. I just wish we could have persuaded him to stop *wanting* to."

In the back, someone started singing. David, anticipating more beer on the wall, covered his ears.

Merry began to smile. "Listen!" she cried, pulling David's hands down.

The kids sang:

> "I have decided to follow Jesus,
> No turning back, no turning back. . . ."

"How about that!" David marveled.

When the camp bus pulled in on schedule, most parents were already waiting at the parking lot. As always, though, there were a few stragglers. It was long after eight when Merry and David, having watched the last parents bundle their child safely into the family car, were free to go.

Merry unlocked her car, stowed her gear in the back and drove home. By now, she reasoned, her parents would have gone to the stadium, where city firefighters and veterans' organizations combined resources annually to provide a patriotic concert and fireworks display.

On the front doorstep she dropped her suitcase and sleeping bag and fumbled for her key. She had the key in the lock before she noticed that the door was not only unlocked, but not even closed. Someone must have stayed behind.

She stepped inside and called, "Mom! Dad! I'm home."

Silence.

Merry thought it odd that the house was open. Her mother, while alarmingly casual where security matters were concerned, always locked the front door when she left the house.

Merry stood still and let her senses test the quiet. She was aware of the beating of her heart, but tried to slow it as she thought over her situation. She was not in the city, where fear could wait in an unlocked house. She was at home in Prairie Chapel. Still, she couldn't rid herself of the sense of dread.

Finally she forced herself to tour the house room by room, turning on lights and opening closets. She didn't find anything suspicious. Afterward she returned to the hall, picked up her gear and went upstairs. This time, when she entered her room, she noticed the note propped up on her dressing table.

Welcome home! We've gone to the Fourth of July program. We'll sit on the south side. Join us if you can; we'll watch for you. If you haven't had dinner, there's some good thick soup on the stove. Love, Mom.

P.S. Jess called to say he's getting up a crowd to go

to the club for the dance and fireworks display. Starts at nine. Said he would call later, and come by for you if you want to go.

Merry looked at the clock. Quarter till nine. Jess would have given up by now. She sighed. She was still shaken by the sense of profound unease that had assailed her in the unlocked house. She would have welcomed Jess's reassuring presence. Oh well. She was dusty and tired, and her hair needed shampooing. It would have taken an hour to make herself presentable.

She comforted herself with a leisurely bath and shampoo. Then she went to Libby's old room, which opened onto the rear balcony. The night was warm and clear, ablaze with stars. Merry put a chair on the balcony and sat there, brushing her hair and watching the aerial displays, now visible on the horizon in the direction of the club.

She fell into a doze, but awakened when she heard a car drive up. The sound of her parents' voices, lifted in cheerful conversation, drifted up from the front walk. Merry ran happily downstairs to greet them.

By long-established habit, they gathered around the kitchen table to visit. Merry was hungry now and remembered the soup her mother had left for her. It gave forth an appetizing odor as she reheated it, and her father decided to join her and have another bowl.

Merry had almost completed her report on camp before she remembered to say, "Do you know you left the front door unlocked this evening?"

There was immediate objection. Her father distinctly remembered snapping the lock before he went outside.

"But then the telephone rang just as we got out the door," recalled Mrs. Conner, "and I thought it might be you, Merry. It was Jess, you know. I added a P.S. to my note. Then I ran downstairs. I thought I snapped the lock and slammed the door—you were rushing me,'' she said reproachfully to her husband.

"It probably didn't catch when you slammed it,'' her husband said soothingly. "Anyway, no harm done. Nothing was disturbed, was it?''

"Not that I noticed,'' Merry said. "I did tour the house.''

"We don't own anything very valuable,'' said Dan Conner.

"Except Mother's jewelry,'' Merry said, and then noticed her mother thinking this over.

"I think I'll just go take a look,'' she decided, bounding up the stairs. She came back downstairs with her face white as chalk. "It's gone.''

They all flew upstairs to stare at the empty chest atop the dresser, and then, futilely, to paw through drawers and look in places the jewelry had never been.

"Why are we doing this?'' Merry cried suddenly. "We shouldn't be touching anything. We should be calling the police!''

"The *police!*'' her mother repeated incredulously, looking as if Merry had suggested something not quite respectable.

"Yes, you're right,'' Mr. Conner decided. "That's the thing to do, of course. We should have called them immediately.''

Officers O'Donnell and Hanratty, having surveyed the scene, sat down at the kitchen table. They accepted coffee and began to ask searching questions. Merry remembered Officer O'Donnell as a mighty upperclassman in high school. Officer Hanratty was a contemporary of Libby's, and a woman.

Mrs. Conner was calm and well controlled, but she still wore a heartbroken look that didn't go unnoticed by her husband and daughter. "It was just some old jewelry," she said. "Very old-fashioned settings. They'd been handed down in my family."

"Describe it, please," said Officer O'Donnell, scratching away with his pen on a complicated-looking form.

Mrs. Conner enumerated her missing jewelry piece by piece, identifying the stones and precious metals.

"Have you had it appraised?"

"No." Mrs. Conner looked surprised. "Why would I do that?"

"For insurance purposes. Do you have insurance?"

"Our house policy includes burglary, with, uh, certain exclusions," Mr. Conner put in.

The policeman looked sympathetic.

"Do you think these few pieces would be worth enough for someone to take the risk of stealing them?" cried Mrs. Conner.

"It's pretty obvious someone has," said the young officer. "I think your jewelry has become quite valuable, Mrs. Conner, especially since you mentioned the heavy, old-fashioned design. That usually means a lot of gold."

"Do you expect to recover it?" Merry challenged.

"Of course we hope to. But we haven't had much luck so far with missing jewelry," said Officer O'Donnell.

"Do you mean there have been other jewelry thefts in Prairie Chapel?" Merry asked.

"Quite a rash of them lately," the policeman replied.

His partner chimed in. "This is the first one we've been able to pin down for sure as a robbery, though, Ed," she reminded him.

"True. Several people up on the hill have reported pieces of jewelry missing. But they can't say when or how the stuff disappeared, or, in some cases, how long it's been gone. We've had no evidence of breaking and entering, and we've got nothing to go on. Not a single set of fingerprints."

"Then how do you know those were thefts?" Merry pursued.

"We don't know," said both officers in concert.

"But you think so," Merry guessed. "Why?"

"Call it woman's intuition," said Officer Hanratty, smiling.

Ed O'Donnell went on, "This time we *know* it was a theft, and exactly when it occurred. You said you looked at the jewelry and decided against wearing it just before you left at seven-thirty for the fireworks display. Your daughter arrived at eight-forty. It appears that someone either knows your habits, or, in this instance, was watching closely."

Mrs. Conner spoke up with spirit. "Young man, I know every one of my neighbors, and have for years. If you suspect any of them, you're wasting your time."

"Actually, we think it's an outsider, someone fairly professional," the young man responded mildly. "Amateurs disturb things and usually leave a trail. They're much easier to catch than professionals, who learn to be both inconspicuous and tremendously observant. If the jewelry reported missing has all been stolen by the same person, he's a thief of impeccable taste. He chooses only the finest."

The doorbell rang. "That'll be the fingerprint man," Officer Hanratty said, moving to open the door.

The third officer proved as courteous and soft-spoken

as the other two. He produced his kit, apologizing in advance for the residue of black powder that would of necessity be left on doorframes and knobs, drawer edges and jewelry boxes. After a while he came back to the kitchen and eyed the other officers.

"Nothing?" they asked in unison.

"Nothing. Either he managed not to touch anything, or he was nicely gloved."

"Wouldn't you think someone running around in gloves on a July night in Prairie Chapel would attract attention?" Merry asked with surprise.

"I'm sure he'd have them off as soon as he was out the door," said Peggy Hanratty. "Besides, who would see him? Everyone in town goes to the celebration."

Officer O'Donnell looked sympathetically at the silent Mrs. Conner. "Here's a card with my name and number where I can be reached. If any of you think of anything that might help us, you let us know."

The doorbell rang again, urgently.

"Who can that be, at this hour?" Mrs. Conner wondered. "It's after midnight!"

Merry answered the door and felt comfort at the sight of Jess.

"Merry!" he cried on a note of relief. "Is anything wrong?"

"Oh, Jess! Mother's been robbed!"

As they went to join the group in the kitchen, Jess put a consoling arm around her. "I drove by to see if you'd gotten home, Merry, and saw those police cars," he said. "Gave me a scare. What was taken?"

After telling him, Merry went on, "They say it happened between seven-thirty and eight-forty, when I came home," she said. "If you had come by for me, you might have seen him! You *didn't* drive by here, did you?''

The police, on their way out, paused to hear his answer.

"No, I intended to, but I got sidetracked. Sally's car wouldn't start, and she was late, so I wound up taking her to the Hideaway. I called you again from out there—it must have been just minutes before you walked in the door. When you didn't answer, I thought it was no use driving all the way back, so I went on out to the club.''

"Too bad," Merry said. "I guess he had a clear field. All the neighbors were probably gone to the fireworks display by then.''

After the police officers took their leave, Jess sympathized with Merry's dazed mother.

"At least it will teach us to keep our doors locked," Mrs. Conner said. "Imagine! In Prairie Chapel!''

"Mr. Conner, when we were over here, I tried to talk you into dead-bolt locks on every door. I'd still like to install them," Jess said. "They don't cost that much.''

"There's nothing of value left to steal," said Mrs. Conner. "I don't have sterling, and we never have gone in for fancy gadgets.''

"There's the television," suggested Mr. Conner. "But it would take a block and tackle to get it out of the den.''

"I don't like to alarm you, but I wasn't thinking about theft," Jess went on. "What I don't like is the idea that Merry walked in here tonight by herself, and someone could very well have been waiting for her.''

Merry tightly clutched Jess's arm.

"I think you're right," Mr. Conner agreed. "Come

over tomorrow afternoon, Jess, and we'll talk about dead-bolt locks and anything else we need to do to improve security.''

"All right, sir, I will. I'll be going now. I'm really sorry about this; hope you get your nice things back, Mrs. Conner. Good night.''

He moved swiftly out of the kitchen, toward the front door, and Merry followed, fighting tears. "This thing tonight has shattered my nerves,'' she confessed.

Jess stopped and turned toward her. "I know,'' he said gently. "Look, I work with some people who . . . know a bit about the seamy side of life. I'll see if I can find out anything.''

"Would you, Jess? I'd be so grateful.''

"I don't know that anything will come of it.''

"I understand. But it'll be encouraging to Mom to know you're trying. Jess . . . you don't have to rush off.''

"I'd like to stay, but I promised Sally a ride home.''

"Oh, of course.'' Always Sally. Merry's hopes fell. "It was good of you to come by. Good night.''

"Good night, Merry. Lock your door.''

After locking the door and saying good night to her parents, Merry went upstairs and sat down at the dressing table to consider her hurt feelings.

Jess was a good friend, but time after time he had made it clear that Sally came first. She must get him out of her mind.

Chapter Seven

August sessions at Camp O'Clouds had a special feature. After a typically dry July, the rains came, settling the dust on forest trails, reducing the fire hazard—and taxing the ingenuity of the counselors, who had to schedule around the late afternoon and evening thundershowers.

That summer, the weather ran true to form. Each morning the campers would awaken to skies of purest blue, sun-gilded and innocent of clouds from horizon to horizon. Before noon fat clouds would come trooping, joining other puffy battalions to take over the blue field. They might reconnoiter for a few hours, spitting and threatening, but ordinarily there was no retreat until at least one camp-soaking maneuver had been executed. In midweek the clouds laid siege. They opened fire with a salvo of hail, then pelted the site with rain from Tuesday noon until Wednesday night.

Taking all this in stride, the Mastersons rescheduled afternoon sports for morning, devotions and study for afternoon. Campfire was moved to the mess hall fireplace, with teenagers crowded in to overflowing. The tireless college counselors worked overtime teaching songs, games and crafts and planning "coffee house" programs.

Traditional events such as the great cookout and the trek to the top of Old Baldy were postponed from day to day.

The next to the last day of the camp session brought heady news from Scout, who monitored the weather reports. Clear and sunny skies were predicted for the rest of the week.

By nine-thirty in the morning every able-bodied camper had hit the trail. All had been well briefed and were suitably dressed and shod—the latter circumstances a testimonial to the devotion and determination of the adult counselors.

"How do you think it's going?" Merry asked David, as they moved side by side along the easy meadow trail that preceded the stiff climb up the mountain.

"All right so far," said David, with characteristic caution. "I do wish, sometimes, that I could be cloned. I have twenty-five boys in that building, and only one other counselor. He starts snoring as soon as the lights go off. That leaves me playing Bed Check Charlie for twenty-five kids, half of whom I don't really know."

"You've got one thing going for you: it's rained buckets the last two nights," commented Merry. "My girls even managed without the usual hourly trips to the latrines."

"We're supposed to have clear skies and a full moon

tonight," David warned. "We'd better drown ourselves in coffee. We'll be bushed from the hike."

"So will the kids," Merry ventured hopefully.

They caught up with Julie Martin, meandering across the meadow hand in hand with a Texas boy named Mac Randall.

"Shake a leg, you two," said David. "You're falling behind."

"You're behinder than we are," Julie said smartly.

"That's a prerogative of age," David retorted. "March!"

Julie and Mac scuttled up the trail, giggling.

"Is Mac in the Dallas group?" Merry wanted to know.

"Mac isn't in any group; I just inherited him," David said. "His pastor is a friend of the Mastersons and talked them into taking him. He arrived in his own fancy car—something I wouldn't have allowed. Paul put him in the big cabin in the hopes of getting him to relate to his peer group. He was a total loner until Julie came."

"He seems to be making up for lost time," Merry said dryly. "Julie talks of nothing else. It seems they've discovered a grand passion. Just think, in four days!"

David shrugged. "It could happen in four minutes," he said.

Merry was surprised into silence.

"Love at first sight it's called. I would have sneered at that idea a year ago," David went on. "Then I looked across our social hall and saw Sally. I know it sounds like the world's dumbest cliché, but it happened to me. My heart stood still."

Merry blinked back sudden tears. After a moment she said gently, "It doesn't sound dumb at all." What it did sound, to Merry, was tragic. Poor David, conscientious- ly doing a job that did not come easily to him, while carrying the burden of an unrequited first love! The whole idea struck painfully close to home. Merry brooded about it all the way up the mountain.

The final steep slope leading to Old Baldy's stony crown was iced with a thin frosting of unmelted snow. Scout had decreed a stop at this point, since he consid- ered a climb to the summit too dangerous for the ill-equipped and uninitiated flatlanders. However, he had no objection to a snow frolic. The campers fell upon the frosty field and played until frozen fingers and sodden socks suggested a retreat to lower levels.

By now the sun was high in the sky, and the thought of lunch brought everyone scampering down the slope to the picnic area. The Camp O'Clouds four-wheel-drive vehicle was waiting there with hot cocoa, sandwiches and fruit. Mike Kenner, who had ridden up with the kitchen crew and a couple of others unable to hike, was wheeling around the grounds in his chair, gathering wood for the cheery fire already roaring in the big fire pit. Hikers crowded around to warm their hands.

"Mike, how did you all manage this?" Merry cried. "The wood must be soaking!"

"I cannot tell a lie; we brought enough dry wood out from camp to get a fire started," Mike said. "But this wood dries out quickly now the fire is going."

The group fell upon the lunch and dispatched it in minutes. Ordered to rest before undertaking the long hike back, they beguiled the time by feeding scraps to the chipmunks, who claimed the picnic area as their feeding ground.

"Don't give them that!" Julie cried when Mike

proffered a portion of tuna sandwich. "Chipmunks are herbivorous."

"Chipmunks are omnivorous, like bears," Mike argued. "They'll eat anything."

The chipmunk settled the argument by sitting up with the tuna sandwich in his two front paws, and eating it before Mike and Julie could say anything further.

"I'm sure I read it in a book," said Julie, who hated to concede a point.

"The chipmunk probably didn't read the book," said Mike.

Others in the Prairie Chapel contingent had launched a conversation obviously designed to badger David: they were speculating about what type of behavior would, or would not, result in their being sent home.

"The contract is pretty ambiguous," a camper called Kevin remarked.

David, who didn't realize where this conversation was headed, rose to the bait.

"It isn't ambiguous at all," he argued. "The rules are plainly stated, and you are told exactly what to bring."

"But we aren't told what *not* to bring," argued Kevin. "It says 'inappropriate items.' How are kids supposed to know what's inappropriate? Why didn't you list 'em?"

"Ha. That would be like telling you not to put beans in your ears. Besides, every one of you knows what's inappropriate to bring to camp."

"Four-inch heels," said one of the girls.

"Booze," said Kevin.

"Sidearms," cried another boy, getting creative. "Nukes!"

"Scandalous magazines," suggested Julie, who was again holding hands with Mac Randall.

"Scandalous magazines would probably just get confiscated," Mike said wisely. "You'd be looked at askance, but not sent home. Right, David?"

David cast up his eyes, then sent a look of fervent hope across the campfire to a grinning Scout.

"It's time to start back," David announced, getting to his feet. "Hi, hi, everybody up and at 'em!"

The troops, with energy renewed in the wonderful way of youth, were moving along the winding trail at a pace that Scout insisted be held *under* a sprint, and looking like a ragged but colorful conga line moving down the mountain.

The moonlit evening was not to be wasted. Returning hikers found preparations under way for a cookout and celebration that proved a huge success.

It had been a big day, so the bedlam that normally accompanied bedtime preparations was subdued to a mere buzz. They all, even the most lively teenagers, seemed to have exhausted their second wind. When taps sounded over the camp, it echoed in a profound and peaceful stillness.

Merry never knew what woke her. Perhaps a sound, perhaps only teacher's instinct, but for a matter of moments she lay in the quiet darkness, hearing nothing, seeing nothing, yet still prey to a growing conviction that someone was missing.

She glided out of bed and lightly tested the lump in each cot. One had no substance. Julie was gone.

Merry willed herself to sit still on her own cot for a few minutes. Julie might have gone to the communal rest room at the edge of the girls' cabin area.

After a few minutes she drew on pants, sweater, jacket, and boots over her pajamas. She seized her flashlight and hurried up the trail to the latrines, to find they were empty.

A sudden suspicion caused Merry to run swiftly down the trail to David's dormitory cabin. The moon bathed the trail in silvery light, so that by leaving her flashlight off and running on tiptoe, she could move through the camp like a ghost. She reached the screened window of the cabin by which, according to prior arrangement, an adult counselor always slept.

"David," she hissed, projecting a stage whisper.

An answering snore was wafted gently back on the night air.

Merry ran around to the other window and tried again. Presently a sleepy voice answered, "Ho. Merry . . . ? Just a minute." In less time than that he appeared at the window.

"Julie's missing," Merry whispered tensely. "Check Mac's bed." Not a minute later David joined her outside, fully clothed over his pajamas.

"Sure enough, he's gone," David said, buttoning his coat. "I have no idea where to look. We'd better get Paul and Scout."

"Please, not yet," Merry whispered urgently. *"I* have an idea where to look. Follow me."

She raced through the moon-bathed camp like a deer, David running to keep up.

When they were out of range of the sleeping quarters, he caught her arm.

"Would you mind telling me where we're going?" he asked.

Merry slowed her pace to stay close to him. "Do you remember the outcropping on the side of the slope that we call Twilight Chapel?" she asked, keeping her voice low. "There's a natural seat like a pew, and a standing rock in front, like a pulpit."

"Yes, I know where that is."

"A few hundred yards beyond, around the next ridge, there's a formation you probably haven't seen, because it's hidden by trees and brush. If you know where it is, you can slip through to it along the canyon wall. There's another natural seat that overlooks the valley. It's hidden from sight on three sides. It's called Lovers' Look. I'm sure generations of twosomes have discovered it and made it their personal hideaway."

David murmured, "You show a suspicious familiarity with the subject."

"I wasn't as reckless as Julie and Mac are," Merry said crisply. "Jess and I used to go up there during free time. We thought we were being rather daring, even at that."

By now Merry and David had gained the top of the hill and started down the other side. Merry, leading the way, angled off to a spot where a moon-silvered pine stood knee-deep in tangled foliage.

"Here," she said, holding branches aside and snapping on her flashlight to show David the pathway. "David, I don't want to frighten the kids. I'm going to call out."

And so she did, loud and clear: "Julie! Mac!"

The silence was profound.

David whispered, "They may not be here."

"They're here all right," said Merry.

She started down the tiny path behind the pine tree, emerging minutes later at the outcropping. Julie and Mac had withdrawn to the far end of the natural seat. Julie crouched there; Mac had instinctively placed himself in front of her, like a lion cub at bay.

"We weren't doing anything," he said hoarsely.

Merry had turned off the flashlight as soon as they were out of the brush. But the moon searched out and illuminated the two young faces, Mac's tense but stubborn, Julie's frightened.

Julie looked past Merry, at David. "There's no use telling him, Mac," she said despairingly. "He won't believe you."

David stood looking down at them. He took a seat on the stone bench, drawing Merry down beside him. He turned to face the two youngsters.

"Try me," he suggested.

"We're in love," the boy announced, pronouncing the words carefully, as if he had just invented them and was trying them out. "I know it might be hard for you to take that seriously, because, sure, we've only known each other four days. But, see, we *know*. We knew right away. And now, suddenly, it's Thursday, and we only have one more day. We needed to be together. Alone together, so we could talk about our future."

"He doesn't care about us and our future," Julie croaked. Her tears spilled over before she turned on David. "You didn't get much love and acceptance while you were growing up, did you? Well then, you ought to know what it's like. If you ever find somebody who loves you just the way you are, you'll try to find ways to be with her. Even if it makes other people . . . think unfair things . . . that aren't true!"

Crying hard, she flung herself on Merry.

"Oh, Merry, Merry, don't let him send me home!" she wailed.

Merry held her, feeling Julie's hot tears sliding down her own neck. She looked despairingly over her head at

David. What could she say to him? The rule on curfew was plain and clear.

"Nobody's thinking unfair and untrue things," she said, stroking Julie's hair. "What we're thinking is that we can't let youngsters run loose on the mountain in the middle of the night. It wouldn't even be safe! Parents would think we'd taken leave of our senses. They'd close down this camp, and rightly so."

Julie raised her head to look at Merry. "I never slipped out before, and I've been coming up here for four years," she reasoned. "This was sort of an emergency. Can't you understand?"

"I do understand how you feel," Merry said earnestly, "but I want *you* to understand why we can't allow it."

"Well, I think we've heard enough," David said sternly.

All conversation ceased. Three pairs of eyes fastened apprehensively on David, the red-bearded Nemesis in the blue jacket.

"First off," he began, "Julie and Mac, if you pull another such trick as this, you *will* be sent home, and that means, right up to the moment of departure. You so much as *bend* the rules again, and I'll find a way to make an example of you, believe me. One time I can chalk up to emotion and immature judgment. Not another. You may consider yourselves on probation."

The other three stared at David in silence, hardly daring to believe the full import of his words.

Finally Julie whispered, "Does that mean you're *not* going to send us home now?"

"Not this time," said David crisply. "You are both on kitchen duty all day tomorrow. That will take care of togetherness for an hour after every meal. You may study together outside, but within sight of the counselors' office, during free time. Your assignment is the third chapter of Ecclesiastes, verses 1 through 8, plus verse 14. You will memorize the passage, and be ready to say it for me when I check with you at four. We'll discuss it at that time. Is that clear?''

Mac said, with lightening countenance, ''Yes, sir!''

David went on, ''We will now go back to our cabins and fall into bed. With as little disturbance as possible, if you please.''

Mac hung back.

''One thing. Do you have to . . . I mean, is it absolutely necessary for you to report this to Reverend Paul?''

''No,'' David said levelly. ''I'm not going to tell anyone about this caper. I'm just as ashamed of it as you are.''

During the exchange between David and Mac, Julie had not taken her eyes off David's face. Now she moved out of Merry's arms and planted herself in front of him.

She cleared her throat. ''David,'' she said unsteadily. ''David, I know we were wrong. Thank you for not sending us home.''

David looked down at her, and favored her with that sudden, knee-weakening smile. ''It would have broken my heart,'' he said earnestly.

Julie's tears spilled over again. Impulsively she threw her arms around his neck. David hugged her, awkwardly patting the fuzzy hood of her jacket. Merry, wet-eyed herself, waited in that moonlit forest glade, watching the walls come tumbling down.

Chapter Eight

Steve arrived at Jess's apartment a little before nine on a Friday evening.

"Are your parents with you?" Jess asked as he opened the door.

"No, they're still at your parents' house, finishing dinner," Steve said. "I thought we might want to do something later, so I encouraged them to come together. Does Sally know?"

"She knows we're coming. She doesn't know there's any special reason. No need to raise false hopes."

"What do you mean, false hopes? She's a shoo-in. I don't know why we didn't think of this before."

"There wasn't any need. Nor an opportunity, until Marvin went to Houston. Marv was a *fixture* out there; one of the best entertainers the club ever had, but now he's gone for good. The Lord moves in mysterious ways! By the way, Steve, you may have to cover for me for a while. One of my kids is coming by here to talk. He said just for a few minutes, but you never know.''

"Couldn't have picked a worse time," Steve groused.

"Oh yes he could have," Jess said cheerfully. "They stay up nights figuring out worse times. Do you want to go on down there and wait for the parents, and tell them I've been held up?"

"Why don't I call them and tell them to meet us at ten? Then I can hole up in your room until you're through," Steve said.

"Suit yourself," said Jess.

Steve headed for Jess's bedroom, taking care to provide himself with a couple of news magazines and a book from the floor-to-ceiling shelves in the living room. Jess's bedroom was small and spartan in arrangement. Steve had been obliged to retire there on another such occasion and found himself bored before half an hour had passed.

Steve had just completed his call to their parents when he heard the doorbell. He checked the bedroom door, which appeared to be closed but was only ajar. Steve retired to Jess's bed with his book and magazines, but he didn't have to open them before Jess's visitor's voice, raised in complaint, carried into the bedroom. Steve was now provided with a fascinating insight into what it meant to be a young man with a record, trying to stay out of trouble.

"I don't know why they keep hassling me," whined Jess's kid, who sounded as if he was within a couple of years of Jess's own age. "I've stayed clean ever since I got out of jail."

"I believe you," Jess said. "You take both cream and sugar, don't you? Here, help yourself. Bobbie, listen. Just because the police ask you about a robbery doesn't mean they assume you did it. It's just as likely they were hoping you might have heard something that would give them a lead."

"Well, I haven't heard a thing. The guys I know, they think someone from the outside did it. Probably slipped in here and heisted the stuff, then fenced it somewhere out of town."

"Where would you suppose they'd go to fence it?"

"Aw, it could be Wichita or Oklahoma City or even Dallas, you can't tell. They could even ship it to Chicago or New York."

"Too bad," Jess said. "The lady who was robbed on the Fourth of July is a special friend of mine."

"No kiddin'." There was a silence punctuated only by the clink of a coffee mug. "That's the one they asked me about, Jess. You remember I was working with you on your girl friend's car. Must've been nearly eight-thirty when I left you. That's what I told the cops. They call you?"

"No. I guess they believed you. You don't have any problem, Bobbie. I know where you were, and I'd tell them, of course. How about another cup?"

"Sounds good." The voice sounded more cheerful. "Tell you what, Jess, if I was looking for Mrs. Conner's jewelry, there're two or three places I'd watch. Might not show up for a while, though. The stuff is too hot. . . ."

With that, he proceeded to rattle off the names of certain business establishments in Wichita, Oklahoma City and Dallas. . . .

The Wittmers and the Browns pronounced themselves enchanted with "Sally's Sing-along" and proved it by staying through the midnight stint. Prompted by their sons, the two couples waited to meet Sally afterward and lavished gracious compliments on her before taking their leave.

Steve and Jess watched them go in silent dismay. If any of the four had thought of Sally in connection with the job at the country club, they hadn't mentioned it.

The young men went to Sally's and helped her finish a whole apple pie, maintaining such a cheerless mien that Sally was moved to ask if they'd received bad news that day.

"Not really," Jess responded, "I just don't believe in allowing idle chatter to interfere with my pie eating."

Steve picked up on Jess's diversionary tactic with a ploy of his own. "Quiet," he commanded, brandishing his fork. "Let nothing be heard but the murmur of moving mandibles."

"What is *that?*" queried Sally, bemused.

"That," Jess lectured, "is an example of apt alliteration's artful aid, shaping a sensational sentence to salute a pastry of unparalleled perfection."

"Virtuoso verbiage," Steve approved.

"You guys *stop!*" Sally laughed. "You know I'm no good at word games. Anyway, I'm glad you're okay, because I'm feeling fine. Do you know what day it is?"

Steve looked blank. Jess consulted his digital watch. "August sixth," he said.

"No, I mean it's *Friday.*"

"As in T-G-I-F?"

"No, at least not in the usual sense. Friday is the last day of church camp and David will be home tomorrow evening. And Merry, of course."

"Oh wow," muttered Steve.

Jess smiled at Sally. "Did it seem a long week?" he asked.

"Endless. I'll bet it's fun at camp, from the little glimpse we got. I never got to go when I was growing up."

"I never wanted to," said Steve.

"It was really a great experience," Jess said. "You could have gone then, Sally, if you had just let Friar Tuck know you wanted to go."

"Doesn't it cost money?"

"There are scholarships."

"Mother would never have stood for that."

"Well, it's not too late. You can join the church and volunteer as a counselor."

"I hardly think so," said Sally. "No matter what you say, Jess, it just wouldn't be suitable."

"According to who? I don't want to hear any more of this," snapped Steve, clapping his hands over his ears.

"You don't understand," said Sally. She rested her forehead in her palms, covering her eyes.

Jess surveyed the other two and laughed out loud. They looked at him. "All I have to do is put my hand over my mouth, and we've got the three monkeys," he pointed out. "We must be retrogressing. I suggest we bag it for tonight."

The next day, Jess waited in vain for an encouraging word from his parents. He'd been invited over for brunch, and the meal was a pleasant one, but no mention was made of Sally's performance the night before. When his stepfather moved out to the sun deck to smoke, Jess followed him. "Mind if I join you?" he asked.

"Pleasure," said Harry Brown.

Jess tackled the subject directly. "When I took you to hear Sally last night, I was hoping you and Mr. Wittmer might consider her for the job as pianist in the club dining room," he said.

"So far as I know, she hasn't applied," said Harry.

"I'm sure she doesn't know the job is open."

"You're welcome to tell her."

"I'm honestly afraid to, unless there's a good chance she can have it, Harry. It would mean so much to her. Sally's had a lot of disappointments in her life. She doesn't need any more."

Harry spent some time filling his pipe with tobacco. When the pipe was full and the tobacco tamped down, he lit it, took it out of his mouth and leaned back to admire it, not smoking but inhaling the fragrance from afar, as if it were incense.

Jess suddenly found himself the cynosure of a pair of particularly shrewd gray eyes. "Are you thinking that if Sally was employed at the club, it would remove your mother's objections to her?" he inquired.

Jess flushed. "With all due respect, sir, Mother's objections to Sally are neither here nor there," he said.

"I realize that you're over twenty-one, Jess, but I would expect that your mother's opinion would be of some interest to you."

"It is," Jess agreed. "But in the case of Sally, it simply hasn't arisen. Sally and I are close friends, and we've supported each other through personal crises. But she's not in love with me—in fact, she's in love with someone else."

Harry Brown opened his mouth and closed it again. He drew a puff on the pipe. "Well, I suppose you would know," he said, with a touch of humor. "In that case, would you mind telling me why you're so anxious to help Sally out of her job at the Hideaway? It seems to be a good one, as that line of work goes."

"I can tell you part of the reason," Jess said. "Sally has accepted the Lord, and she wants to join the church. The job is a stumbling block. I wouldn't venture an opinion as to whether she's right or wrong to feel that way. Some people right there in the church would undoubtedly feel she's taking a very narrow view. But it's a hang-up for Sally. You may not be aware of it, Harry, but she's the daughter of a rather tragic alcoholic. Died a few years ago. That has a lot to do with it, I think."

"Sounds reasonable." The pipe had gone out; it was necessary for Harry to deal with it again. Jess wondered how anyone ever had the patience to smoke one.

"Do you think I should tell Sally that she should apply?" Jess pursued the subject.

"I think I have a better idea," said Harry Brown. "Wittmer and I are on the board, but Cass Sloan was designated to hire someone for us. Cass has the music company, you know. Would you like me to call him and suggest that he and his wife go and hear Sally?"

"That would be great, Harry."

"I believe she'll do a better job of selling herself than I could possibly do by telling Cass about her," said Harry Brown. "Of course, it remains to be seen whether the salary would be satisfactory, or whether she would even like the job. I think we would just want background music rather than a sing-along, except perhaps on Family Night. And of course, we have a combo out there on Saturday nights."

"I don't think any of that will be a problem."

"Very well, I'll see what I can do. I suggest you not

say anything until we find out what Cass's reaction will be.''

"Of course not."

Harry Brown rose, and Jess immediately got to his feet.

"You don't have to leave. Stick around and see what Cass has to say." Harry laid a hand briefly on his stepson's shoulder. "It's always nice to have you around, Jess," he added.

Jess sat back and stretched out in the deck chair, the late morning sun no less warming than the fond word from his stepfather.

The Sunday morning after their session at camp, Merry and David were absolved from duties. They had arrived at midnight after a bus trip slowed to a crawl by heavy rain. So Friar Tuck's wife took over the Sunday school and her husband preached both services. Nothing was required of David except his presence in the chancel second service to read the Scripture and offer a prayer of thanks for the group's safe return. David was therefore in a position to observe the arrival of Sally Jones.

It was an unprecedented entrance. Sally was walking proudly and her face was beaming. Instead of slipping into a seat somewhere in the back, she arrived glowing in the center aisle, and, catching sight of Merry near the front, murmured to the usher. She was immediately escorted down the aisle, where she waited confidently as the other occupants of the pew moved to make room for her at Merry's side.

During the service Merry sensed that Sally was virtually palpitating with excitement. After a broad smile and hand squeeze for Merry, she had fastened her enormous dark eyes on David, who was already having trouble looking anywhere else. Once, inadvertently intercepting their mutual gaze, Merry turned her eyes away, as one avoiding the brightness of noonday.

After Friar Tuck pronounced the benediction, and the organist woke the echoes with a triumphant Bach Toccata and Fugue, Sally turned and gave Merry a great hug.

"Welcome home!" she cried. Then she whispered excitedly, "Oh, Merry, guess what? I had a phone call this morning from Mr. Sloan. He came to hear me last night and decided to offer me a job playing in the club dining room. Isn't that the most wonderful thing you ever heard?"

"Why, I guess so . . . if *you're* pleased," Merry said cautiously. "What does Jess think of it?"

"I haven't told him yet." Sally stood on tiptoe, looked behind them and then whispered impatiently, "Oh, there's *such* a line to shake hands with David. . . ."

The line eventually diminished. David greeted Sally by taking both of her hands. His eyes shone like blue stars. Sally whispered her news. David looked down at her. Merry began to back away.

"Darling," she heard David murmur, "my office is open. Could you wait for me there? I'll slip away the minute I can. . . ."

Merry, now moving rapidly in the opposite direction, found herself face to face with Jess. He was standing by himself, looking over in the direction of David and Sally. He was smiling, but his eyes were suspiciously moist. He hadn't, apparently, missed a thing.

Merry felt a thrust of actual physical pain in the region of her chest.

Jess's eyes settled on Merry, who immediately

donned a cheery, if impersonal, smile. Jess, she assumed, would wish to keep his feelings private.

"Hi, Merry," he said pleasantly. "How was camp? Lose any more kids?"

"You know the same thing never happens twice. They think up something worse. Sometime I'll tell you about it."

Even as she spoke, she knew she *wouldn't* tell him about it. She would avoid the very mention of Lovers' Look.

"Well, I hope it was an easier week . . . and a more peaceful homecoming." His eyes were kind, but they kept their distance. Merry thought she knew why and ached to comfort him. However, the kindest thing to do, she was sure, was to keep up the pretense of normalcy. Jess must never know that she felt his pain as if it were her own.

"Merry, come in here, please!"

Merry looked up, surprised. She had no sooner arrived at the church and paused to pass the time of day with Anne Moulton, the church secretary, than she heard the summons from the pastor's office.

She raised her eyebrows at Anne and went into the inner office. The Reverend John Barnabus Tucker greeted her and invited her to be seated, then began digging like a terrier through piles of letters, memos, printed material and periodicals. These had been classified into neat stacks earlier by Anne, who fought a losing battle to keep her boss organized. By noon his desk would look as if she'd never touched it.

Friar Tuck, whose mind was considerably more orderly than his desk, eventually extracted the letter he was digging for and handed it to Merry. "Read it—it's from Mrs. Brigham," he said. "Merry, have you signed a contract to teach this year?"

"No," Merry said. "I still can, though. Allison—that's my roommate—called me just yesterday to tell me my job is still available. Our principal had phoned her."

"What have you decided?"

"To be honest, I still *haven't* decided. You know, we had discussed my entering seminary and taking a master's in Christian education. I don't know why I'm taking so long to make up my mind."

"Maybe it's Divine Providence," said Friar Tuck. "As you will see from Estella's letter, she needs an extension. It would be wonderful for us if you could stay on. Of course, the salary isn't as good as what you made teaching, but the spiritual rewards are priceless."

"I'll have to think about it," said Merry. "This is an option I didn't know I had. I was going to ask for some time off this week to go up and talk to my principal. I'll only need a couple of days; Will De Jong has offered to fly me."

"Take all the time you need. This is a quiet month. Before long, though, the pressure will be on. Everything starts running full tilt in September."

"So you really need to know right away, don't you?"

"Well, yes. However, I don't want to pressure you. The situation doesn't give you much job security. Estella hasn't made up her mind what to do. It may become necessary to admit her mother in a nursing home. However, Estella hopes to avoid doing so if possible. Her mother is mentally alert and naturally wants to regain her health and remain in her own home."

"I hope she can. It's so sad when people have to give up their homes."

"Well, that might give you a little extra motivation."

Merry turned to the letter and skimmed it, sympathizing with the conscientious Estella's dilemma. Then she considered her own situation, wondering how long the job here at the church might really be open. There was no question about her preference if this job were permanent! The heavier fall schedule would be all the more challenging.

She looked at Friar Tuck. "I suppose if Mrs. Brigham decided to come back during the next few months, I could enter seminary in January," she said.

"I should think so. But there might be a hiatus. Would that pose a problem?"

"Dad can usually use some extra help in the store," Merry said. "I guess I'd be worth my board and keep. What I really ought to find out is how badly I'm needed at my school. My principal gave Allison the impression he'd have a difficult job replacing me. Not true, of course, but a boost for the ego."

"Well, most likely you'll know by the time you return exactly what you want to do. Today is Wednesday. A week from Friday, there will be a curriculum specialist from our denomination holding an all-day seminar at the church in MacFadden. I'd like you to attend, if you're going to stay."

"I'll plan on it," Merry said. "However, if I do sign a contract, I'll have to leave Prairie Chapel that weekend."

"You decide where you can be of the most service, my dear," Friar Tuck said in parting. "And ask the Lord's help in making your decision."

"I'd like to be happy as well as of service," Merry said wistfully. "I'm afraid I'm not like St. Paul. I haven't learned in all things to be content."

"We can't all be like St. Paul, nor is as much expected of us," said Friar Tuck. "I don't hold with the notion that Christians are supposed to be miserable. Why *shouldn't* you be happy? You're the child of a King."

Merry went back to her own office to think. She'd been avoiding making a decision and wishing she could simply stop the clock and stay right where she was. Friar Tuck had always been a perfect boss. David, shining from dawn to dark with quiet happiness, was increasingly a joy to work with. Will De Jong seemed content to plan her leisure hours, asking nothing more in return than an occasional kiss and her undivided attention.

Now Mrs. Brigham had made it easy for her to do just that: stay put. And yet, so far as finding a direction for her life, she would be marking time.

Merry folded her hands on her desk, and bowed her head. She prayed for guidance in directing her life, asking that she be shown the path she should take.

The rest of the week, it rained. This was no summer shower, but a veritable deluge, with low ceiling and visibility at zero. Will's little bird stayed on the ground.

Just when Merry had decided the Lord was showing her in an unmistakable way, the rain stopped and the ceiling lifted. It wasn't exactly a beautiful day, but Will pronounced it safe for flying.

Merry called Allison to secure an appointment with the principal for her, and hotel reservations for Will. Merry and Will got ready in a hurry and flew north.

As the interview progressed, Merry experienced her old feelings of frustration. Mr. Kyle shared her goals for more effective teaching: smaller classes; brighter, cleaner classrooms; better resource material; more support for regular attendance and more motivation for excellence. Mr. Kyle pursued these goals with hope; he had found no better weapon. Merry thought sadly, nothing is going to change. . . .

Allison was waiting outside in her car.

"Well, what did you decide?" she asked as Merry got in.

"I decided no," said Merry. "It isn't as if I'm leaving him high and dry. He has other applicants."

"Well, don't be defensive; I'm not arguing with you this time," Allison said. "Selfishly, I wanted you to come back. But if I were in your boots, wild horses couldn't drag me."

". . . Away from glamorous Prairie Chapel? I'm glad you've finally seen the light."

"You know very well what I mean. Your Will is the neatest guy you've ever gone with."

"I *thought* you'd like him," Merry said, pleased. "Didn't we have fun last night? He's an adventurous spirit, like you. Incidentally, he isn't 'my' Will."

"He's playing it cool, because you are," Allison guessed shrewdly. "A guy that attractive wouldn't be at your beck and call if he didn't have serious intentions. Don't you care for him?"

"Yes, but I'm not in love with him."

"You mean you can be with that handsome hunk and not feel any physical attraction?"

"I suppose I have it backward for nowadays, but I'd like to get the emotional attraction nailed down before I worry about the physical attraction."

"Oh, come off it, Queen Victoria. You must know by now if the chemistry is right."

"I don't seem to be getting through, roommate. What I mean is, if I decided I was in love with Will, I feel sure the chemistry would take care of itself."

"In love, in love, piffle!" cried Allison. "I think

you're hoping for some adolescent romance with moonlight and roses and stardust. Like you had with what's-his-face.''

Merry was silent. After a moment Allison said in a different voice, "I didn't mean to hurt your feelings."

"I know." Merry sighed. "I was just worrying that you may be right."

That morning Will, who had been out to check the plane and the weather, reported heavy storms to the south, and they didn't leave as scheduled.

"We could probably dodge around, but getting this late a start, I'm a little worried about it," he said.

"If you're worried, I'm panic-stricken," Merry said. "I'll call Friar Tuck and my parents."

Will was in wonderful spirits; he had a rental car and an agenda.

Allison was characteristically ready to drop everything in favor of a new adventure. Less characteristically, she took the trouble to fix an excellent brunch first, and to dress her best for the day.

Wednesday morning was even worse. Again they were grounded, and again Allison and Will collaborated on finding beguiling ways to waste a day.

Thursday morning, the sky was still gray and lowering, but at least it wasn't raining.

"Is it safe to go?" Merry wondered. "I'm supposed to attend a seminar in MacFadden tomorrow."

"It's safe to *start*," Will said cheerily. "As of now, there's decent visibility all the way. If it fogs in again, we can either park the bird or turn back. Want to come along, Allison?"

"As a matter of fact, I'm dying to; I've never flown in a light plane. But I can't leave until after Orientation."

"Give me a holler any weekend; I'll come get you," Will offered.

"Such as, Labor Day weekend," Merry suggested.

"I guess I'm going to have to make the pilgrimage, now that you've made the decision to stay there," Allison allowed.

"Did I make a decision? I feel as if I'm just following the line of least resistance. Anyway, come Labor Day."

"I might. I don't know how I've resisted this long, what with your dazzling accounts of the good life in Prairie Chapel. Anyway, if I come, I'll fly commercially."

"Better let us meet you in Wichita, at least," Will advised. "The connections into Prairie Chapel are lousy. Just two shuttle flights a day for businessmen."

"Okay, I'll call you," Allison conceded. "I'll miss you, Merry. And now I'll have to break down and find a new roommate."

The two friends exchanged a big hug before parting. Will clamored for—and got—equal treatment.

They flew home, skipping over and around storms, but without incident.

"Mighty wet down there," Will observed. "All those fields are standing in water."

"Fortunately they've already harvested the wheat," Merry said. "We need our rains in the spring, not at harvesttime."

"Got rain on both ends this year. Many more days like the last few, and we'll have some serious flooding."

"It only floods in the spring," Merry said, unconsciously repeating the conventional wisdom of the area. "We used to have the whole south end of Prairie Chapel underwater every few years, when the Arkansas River flooded. I suppose the Kaw Dam has helped flood control. Anyway, we haven't had to worry since they built a big federal highway between us and the river. It makes a natural dike.''

"So Prairie Chapel never gets flooded anymore?"

"Not in years. I'm sure the people who live in the lower end of town are thankful. Our house is on high ground, so we never did suffer. Libby and I used to think it was exciting, shame on us! We'd sneak off and watch the men sandbagging the old road. There was a rickety bridge over the river then, which made a lot of noise when you went over it. Libby and I called it the Trip-Trop Bridge—you know, as in 'The Billy Goats Gruff.' In floodtime the river would rise and be knocking against that bridge with uprooted trees and floating houses. Finally the bridge just collapsed.''

"Did you see that happen?"

"Almost! Libby heard about the danger, on the radio. We were on our way, but Mother sent Dad after us. I missed my one chance to be present at a real disaster.''

Will waved his hand toward the horizon. "See anything familiar out there?"

"Looks like the tank farm. Oh, and the refinery."

"Good navigation. We'll soon be on approach. Not a minute *too* soon! Getting dark fast. I'm glad we didn't stop for supper. We'll grab a bite on the way home.''

Prairie Chapel was sodden. Lawns stood in water; every low place had become a puddle, every gutter ran a muddy stream.

"It must have rained the entire time we were gone," Merry exclaimed as they forded the parking lot at Handy Andy's Hamburgers.

"More to come, from the looks of the sky," Will said. "This is one time I'm glad to be on the ground."

They wolfed hamburgers and chili. As Will was paying the cashier, Merry was surprised to notice Jess at a table in the rear of the room.

He was listening intently to one of his two young companions and apparently had not noticed Merry and Will. Merry studied the boy talking to Jess. He had shiny black hair and a swarthy complexion; his black T-shirt and pants emphasized his thinness. The other was a contrast: sandy-haired, with thick neck, powerful shoulders and great freckled arms. Both looked tough.

Merry tried to catch Jess's eye in order to wave a greeting. But Jess didn't look up. Apparently he was engrossed in a very private conversation.

Will took Merry's arm and tucked it in his own. As they drove home in gathering darkness, it began to drizzle.

Noting the smudges of fatigue under Merry's eyes, Will didn't attempt to linger. Stopping long enough to check in with her parents, Merry told her mother not to fix breakfast, since the conference was to begin with a get-acquainted snack. Merry set her alarm, then went straight to bed, planning to slip out early the next morning in order to be in MacFadden in time for the continental breakfast.

She went to sleep immediately and stayed soundly and peacefully asleep through hour after hour of steady rain.

Chapter Nine

Merry opened the front door on an August morning so darkly overcast that, save for the heat, it could have been November.

Although it wasn't raining when she left home, after one look at the sky, Merry provided herself with a waterproof hat and slicker. She'd already opted for boots and a pantsuit rather than the tailored dresses she usually chose for church meetings.

Taking care not to wake anyone, Merry slipped out shortly after seven. Ordinarily the drive to MacFadden would take little more than thirty minutes, but today she allowed herself an hour, so that she could proceed down the swamped, narrow roads with extreme caution.

Merry switched on the car radio to enjoy a morning music program; however, it was promptly interrupted by the Highway Patrol, warning of slick road conditions and muddy soft shoulders on State Highway 29. Since this was the very road Merry was traveling, she listened with sharp attention as the patrolman reported that more thundershowers were expected throughout the day.

Ten miles out of MacFadden, she crossed the West Fork River, normally a docile stream that might well have been designated a creek. Today it had achieved full river status. It was running bank to bank and nearly level with the top, a swift and sullen thoroughfare for tons of debris, some of which battered against the bridge before being sucked under by the rapid current. Despite the relative smallness of her station wagon, the bridge creaked and rumbled as the car passed over it. Another Trip-Trop Bridge, Merry thought.

A few minutes later she pulled into the parking lot of the neat white brick ranchstyle church in MacFadden. She was early, but there were several cars already parked. Merry went inside and met the MacFadden education director with several of her teachers. Fresh coffee was brewing, and they were preparing to greet the brave souls who might be venturesome enough to ford the sodden roads to attend the seminar.

Most of those who had signed up actually came, agreeing that since flooding was a spring phenomenon, the weather was duty-bound to clear up without any major inconvenience.

Rolls, coffee and juice were offered while the commuters told harrowing tales of skids, wet brakes and near-disasters. When the curriculum expert arrived, it soon became apparent that the gentleman knew his business well. The group became so absorbed that no one noticed when, halfway through the morning, the rains began again with a vengeance.

Lunch was served promptly at twelve in the social hall. The pastor arrived, looking worried, to give the blessing, and when dessert had been offered, he again got to his feet to announce the news that had been causing him visible agitation.

The authorities had advised that travel on all routes to and from MacFadden was becoming extremely hazardous. It was expected that, although north–south and east–west freeways would remain open, connecting roads would be closed within an hour or two if rains continued.

"For all of you who want to stay and complete the conference, be assured we'll find overnight lodging for you," he continued. "For those who feel you must return home today, it may be better to leave immediately after lunch. If you go, Godspeed—and please, drive carefully!"

He bowed his head and pronounced a heartfelt benediction.

Merry didn't think twice. Already she had been stranded two days out of that week. Being stranded at Allison's was one thing; being stuck overnight in Mac-Fadden was quite another. She thanked her hosts, found her hat and slicker and dashed through the downpour to the rusty blue wagon, carefully protecting her folder under her raincoat.

Negotiating Highway 29 in a cranky old car with water up to its hubcaps proved an unforgettable experience. The car coughed and sputtered and the brakes forgot their function. Merry's instinct told her to creep along at a snail's pace, but the car declined to move at a snail's pace, letting it be known that cars are intended to run, not walk.

When she arrived at the slowest possible speed she could manage without stalling, Merry began to hope that she might actually stay on the road and reach her destination. Ahead, she saw the bridge looming in the gloom. Ten miles had been safely negotiated—almost a third of the way.

Lights flashed red in the area of the bridge. Merry peered through the downpour, groaning silently. If she had to slow down any more, the car was likely to stop for good.

The flashing red lights belonged to a highway patrol car, and it was parked squarely in front of the bridge. Merry had no recourse but to slow and stop. The motor promptly died.

"What's the matter?" Merry called out.

"We've closed the bridge," the patrolman said. "The city engineer was out and pronounced it unsafe. You'll have to go back."

Merry looked across the bridge. A twin patrol car blocked the other end. A large truck was in the process of backing to turn around.

"How in the world will I get to Prairie Chapel?" Merry groaned.

"You can go back to the turnoff just south of Mac-Fadden, and go around by Discovery," said the patrolman. "It's farther, but it's still passable."

Merry tried the starter. Then she tried again . . . and again. The young patrolman bustled up to take charge. He couldn't start it either.

"What do I do now?" Merry appealed in despair.

"Barney and I'll shove it off the road," said the young man. "Next car that comes along, we'll get you a ride back to MacFadden. You can get a tow truck there."

Merry watched her car sink in mud up to its axles as they shoved it off the roadway. Across the bridge, she saw another big truck turning. If she could just run across the bridge, she could flag a ride home. Still, she had better look after her car.

"Get in the patrol car," directed the older man. "Here come a couple of vehicles. I'll see if it's someone I know. Don't want to send you off with just *anybody*."

"Thanks; that's thoughtful," said Merry.

She had her hand on the door of the patrol car, but she never opened it. A sudden deafening sound filled the air—a sound at once indescribable and unforgettable, something between a crack and a roar.

Someone yelled, "The bridge! The bridge is going!"

The oncoming cars stopped in their tracks as the structure, seemingly in slow motion, buckled and caved. People came tumbling out of their vehicles, pointing, gesticulating soundlessly, apparently dumb with shock.

There was a roar as a considerable portion of the superstructure collapsed into the river. Then, suddenly, the river itself was around their feet and Merry heard herself scream.

As quickly, the water receded, leaving the shocked watchers to register a new development. The river, with the collapse of the bridge, had bitten off a sizable chunk of the bank on each side. The very roadbed on which they were standing was fast becoming undermined and in jeopardy.

The patrolmen shouted to the oncoming drivers, waving them back. While the startled motorists were beating a hasty retreat, the officers ran for their own car.

Merry was beside it, standing as if mesmerized, the rain running rivulets down the corners of her hat brim.

The policeman followed her gaze. Her station wagon had been left with its front wheels hanging over the chasm. As they watched, it began to tilt, in agonizing slow motion. In seconds it would be gone.

The thought galvanized Merry, who broke into a swift sprint. Barney, fired with adrenaline, had her in three giant strides.

"Where do you think you're going?" he yelled frantically. "What in blazes do you think you can do?"

The scene flashed again to silence and slow motion. Merry stood stiffly in Barney's grip, watching her car move with eerie deliberation to a position almost on its nose. Then it tumbled over and over into the swift water.

"It's gone," she said, numbly.

"Too bad," he agreed. "It's a shame, honey, but cars are expendable. You have insurance, right? And you're okay; that's what's important. Look, here's another police car. We'll send you back to MacFadden."

That day Jess was thankful for an indoor assignment. He was replacing some rotted wood in the Diederich farmhouse on Route 3. At noon he stopped, ready for a break from the necessary but tedious job.

He climbed into the company's big, high-wheeled truck, which Joe insisted he drive today, since Route 3, alternatively known as State Highway 29, had been underwater a good part of the week.

Jess drove to town, fording water all the way. He parked in front of the Pioneer Café and went inside. He was hailed immediately by Sally and David, who were sitting at a table, openly holding hands. Jess accepted their invitation to join them.

"Did you start your new job?" he asked Sally.

"Yes, on Monday," Sally said, nodding.

"How's it going?"

"Super. Much slower pace than the Hideaway. More casual. I love it."

"I'll try to stop in tonight or tomorrow night."

"Jess, I'd like to take a group of friends out there myself, if you'd let me use your membership and then pay you," David suggested. "People who've entertained me . . . Merry, of course, and Libby and Chris; Will and you and your friend Steve. A regular party. Is something like that allowed?"

"Of course. No problem."

"David was thinking of having his party tomorrow night," Sally put in.

"There's no hurry, since Merry didn't take the job in the city," David reminded her. "We'd been thinking about it partly as a farewell for Merry."

"I knew Merry was gone this week, but I didn't realize she was job-hunting," said Jess.

A note in his voice caught Sally's attention. "I think the job was hunting Merry," she said, watching Jess with interest. "Merry's principal had wanted her to sign her contract to teach next year. So Will flew Merry up to talk about it."

"After which Merry decided she still didn't want to go back," said David with satisfaction. "She's staying with us as long as we need her."

"That should be nice for all concerned," said Jess neutrally.

"Where's Merry today?" asked Sally.

"Don't you remember? She drove to MacFadden early this morning for an all-day seminar," said David.

Jess laid down his fork.

"She drove to MacFadden? In her old car?"

"I guess so. Why? Do you think the roads are getting hazardous?"

"The Highway Patrol has been saying so, about every fifteen minutes. And that car of hers barely runs in the best of circumstances."

Jess seemed to have lost interest in his salad and picked at it distractedly. A moment later he rose, dropping some bills on the table.

"I have to leave, but, David, when you get to your office, would you call the church in MacFadden, get hold of Merry and tell her not to drive home? Tell her to stay put. I'll go over in the truck and get her before they shut down the road completely, which they will at any minute. We can go back for her car when the roads clear."

The restaurant door closed firmly behind him.

David looked at Sally. "Well, well," he said. "Now I know something I never knew before."

"I've known for years."

"Is it mutual?"

"I don't know. It used to be. Merry keeps her feelings to herself. So does Jess, for that matter. But I can always read Jess."

"I'd better make that call," David said. "I'll just do it from the pay phone here, and not wait until I get back to the church, since Jess is so set on it."

He returned from the telephone a few minutes later, looking worried. "I called up there and talked to the pastor," he said. "Merry started home right after they finished lunch."

"Well, I suppose that's best," Sally said. "She'll get home before they close the road. Jess will probably meet her en route."

"That's a cheering thought," said David. "There

aren't many mini-wagons in the world painted the peculiar shade of blue Merry's is. It should be hard to miss.''

As Jess drove down Highway 29, he established radio contact with the construction company office.

"Jan? Put Joe on, will you?" he said.

In a moment he was talking to his boss. Joe approved his mission and promised to telephone Mrs. Diederich to explain the delay on her carpentry. Jess relaxed. The big truck moved ahead, undaunted by several inches of water running across the roadbed. Within twenty minutes he should be in MacFadden.

Instead, within twenty minutes Jess had encountered the highway patrolmen at the West Fork River bridge. In silence he digested the dismaying news: the bridge was closed. He would have to retrace the miles to Prairie Chapel, then go the long way around by Discovery. At least another hour!

Jess wheeled the big truck around and was preparing to start off in the other direction when something in the rearview mirror caught his eye. It was hard to see in the downpour, but he thought he had caught a glimpse of Merry's blue station wagon moving across his line of sight.

Jess pulled the truck off on the shoulder and felt it sink. No matter. He could get it out again. He had to see what was going on at the other side of the bridge. He jumped out of the truck, thinking they wouldn't let him drive across, but perhaps he could sprint.

Jess was never more wrong. At that exact moment he was startled to a standstill by the same alarming noise that had transfixed Merry and the watchers on the other side. Jess, too, stood rooted to the spot, watching the shattering demise of the once sturdy West Fork bridge.

Then Jess saw the sequel: a tiny blue station wagon on the opposite side beginning to nod, then bowing deeply before it took the plunge into the river. Jess's despairing cry drew the attention of the two patrolmen on his side. Not a minute too soon, for Jess was off like a bullet toward the river.

Jess was harder to stop than Merry. It took both patrolmen, and both were briefly in jeopardy, for Jess was a wild man until their insistent message finally got through: *No one in the car! There's no one inside it!*

Jess got hold of himself. "How do you know?" he whispered, panting.

"Radio. Guys on the other side," breathed one of his friendly adversaries. "They got the girl with them. You can talk to her, I expect."

"Please."

Jess looked at his clenched fists in a puzzled way, as if they belonged to someone else. He unclenched them and looked at the two patrolmen. "Sorry," he said.

The younger one said tentatively, "Jess?"

Jess stared at him.

"Oh, hiya, Sam," he said. "Didn't recognize you."

The younger patrolman offered his hand, and when Jess gripped it, clapped him on the shoulder. He led Jess to the car, where the "guys on the other side" gave him their update. They had just packed Merry into a police car and sent her back to MacFadden. They would radio the police dispatcher to tell her he would be coming for her.

Jess went back and started his truck. The four-wheel drive made short work of the mud in which its wheels were mired. Jess pulled back onto the road and soon was trundling along through the downpour, leaving a wake of displaced droplets from each wheel. Curbing his impatience, he held the truck to a sedate pace. He should arrive in MacFadden inside of an hour. Hurrying, he might not get there at all.

Merry's clothing was cold and wet, and she felt confused and tired. The MacFadden police headquarters, acting as clearinghouse for commuters with stalled cars, stranded tourists and anxious relatives, was noisy and crowded. People milled around the desk of the harrassed dispatcher, who was trying with heroic patience to keep everyone calm while giving out all useful information.

Merry sagged in a wooden chair while her wet slicker, which she'd struggled out of, made puddles on the floor. A few blocks away was the church, where she might find a friend and a cup of hot coffee. But the dispatcher had told her to wait: someone was coming for her.

Waiting, she thought it would be her father. In her experience, parents always appeared in a crisis. Still, she wondered how this could be. Her parents weren't expecting her until evening. She had been too dazed at the bridge to tell the patrolmen anything, yet when she had been brought here, they already had a message for her. Perhaps it had been a mistake.

As she was contemplating this disquieting idea, she saw a young man striding toward her, looking utterly familiar yet so unlikely in this place that she had to look again. When she recognized Jess Merry jumped up and ran into his arms.

She had kept herself under careful control, but now

she found herself shaking and crying. "Oh, J-jess," she stammered. "The b-bridge went out and the river took my c-car. . . ."

Jess held her tightly. "I know; I saw it from the other side. For an awful moment I thought you were in it."

"No, I wasn't," Merry explained unnecessarily. "I'm really j-just fine."

And then, because she couldn't control her chattering teeth, she hid her face in Jess's shoulder and cried.

"Hush, hush, don't cry; it's all right now. You're safe with me." Jess spoke gently in her ear, as if she were a child. His hands found and smoothed away the tension in her back and at the base of her neck. His lips found hers and stopped their trembling.

"Jess . . ." Merry raised her head, suddenly aware of her surroundings. "This room is full of people."

"They couldn't care less, Merry. They're all busy with their own problems." He picked up her slicker and helped her into it. "Better wear the hat, too; it's still pouring. Here's your purse. Come on. We have to drive home the long way, and we'd better get going. Highway 29 is closed, of course, with the bridge out. Discovery Creek is almost out of its banks; they'll close that road next, and we'll be stranded."

He took Merry's arm and hurried her out of the station.

"Should you check with the dispatcher?" Merry asked.

"I spoke to him as I came in, so he'd be informed in case your folks call. Anyway, I'll radio Joe and ask him to call them and tell them we're on our way."

They hurried along the street, rain pelting their faces, their boots squelching in standing water. Still, Merry knew a moment of blinding happiness. Jess was here, big and competent and reassuring, taking care of her like a . . . husband. And they were going home.

Out on the highway, Merry peered through the rain-blasted windshield. Water everywhere. At times she couldn't even make out the roadbed. "C-can you s-see anything?" she demanded of Jess.

"If I couldn't, I wouldn't be driving."

"I w-wonder why my t-teeth keep chattering. It isn't that cold, is it?"

"You're probably still having a little shock reaction," Jess said with great calm. "I'll turn on the heater. I wish I could hold you, but the situation demands both my hands on the wheel." He smiled over at her. "Why don't you move over a little closer, and as soon as you feel warm, take off that slicker. It's like cuddling up to a bowl of cornflakes."

Merry managed a watery grin.

The truck's big heater soon warmed the cab. Outside, early darkness began to gather. Fatigue was taking its toll of Merry. She still suspected that Jess was driving blind, and felt it her duty to stay awake and worry about it. Yet she nevertheless nodded and nodded. Finally she sagged against him, deeply asleep.

It was exceptionally dark when the truck pulled up in front of the Conner house. Jess turned and gathered up the sleep-sodden bundle that was Merry, seeking to awaken her gently.

"Merry," he said softly. "Merry, honey. We're home."

At a point between deep sleep and wakefulness, Merry recalled the collapse of the bridge. She gave a despairing cry.

Again Jess spoke tenderly to her, comforting and

caressing, covering her cheek with warm kisses. The frightening image faded, and Merry realized where she was. She turned in Jess's arms, put her own around his neck and kissed him warmly on the mouth.

Jess raised his head and, in the rain-dimmed glow of the streetlight, tried to study her face. "Merry, are you awake? Merry? I'm Jess, you know."

"Mmmmm," said Merry.

"Merry," said Jess urgently, "We need to talk. . . ."

The door of the Conner house opened. Dan Conner stood illuminated in the doorway. He peered anxiously out into the darkness, then reached in his shirt pocket for his glasses and peered again.

Merry, conscience-stricken, cried, "Oh, poor Daddy!"

Jess sighed. Then he reached down and blinked the lights of the truck.

Mr. Conner's face lit up. He disappeared momentarily, then reappeared and came wading across the yard, wearing slicker and boots and carrying a huge black umbrella.

They made a triumphal procession into the house, Dan Conner shielding them both under his big umbrella.

Merry was hugged and cosseted by her mother, father, sister, brother-in-law, nieces and nephew. Her adventures were reviewed and wondered at, her loss mourned. Mrs. Conner insisted on regarding Jess as a hero, despite his embarrassed protests that the highway patrol had done what little rescuing was necessary.

Mrs. Conner had managed to keep relatively calm during the anxious hours by cooking an immense dinner. She hailed everyone to the table.

Jess politely declined. Under the critical scrutiny of

Libby, he had become aware of his work clothes, now wrinkled after being repeatedly rain-soaked and partially dried.

He departed, but not before Merry managed to escape long enough to see him to the door.

"I'd still like to talk to you," he said in a low tone. "All right if I come over tomorrow?"

"Of course. I wish you would." Merry looked up at him, wanting to say more. But Chipper came tagging along behind her. She caught Jess's hand and murmured, "I'll be expecting you."

"Until tomorrow, then."

Jess bent and gave her a hasty kiss.

Chipper seized Merry around the knees. Merry picked him up; she and Jess exchanged a smile over his head. As she went back to join the family, she didn't notice Chipper's weight, and her feet scarcely seemed to touch the carpet. She couldn't remember when, in the past six years, she had been so sublimely happy.

The same deluge that cost Merry her car caused a radical change in plans for Steve Wittmer.

While Merry sat in her meeting at MacFadden, Steve also sat, but in far more luxurious circumstances. He lounged in a silken robe in the family breakfast room, arguing with his mother over a late brunch.

"I just don't think you should be driving to Oklahoma City on a day like this," said Barbara Wittmer.

"Five miles past MacFadden, I catch the freeway, and then it's clear sailing all the way," Steve reminded her.

"But why today of all days?"

"Because," said Steve with exaggerated patience, "today of all days is the day I have an appointment with an investor. I should say, with *the* investor, since none of our fine friends cared to risk a lousy five thousand, and Dad won't even co-sign a loan for me. I really do appreciate the vote of confidence.''

"Well, Dad's backed you for quite a while and has seen no return on investment," his mother pointed out. "As for our friends, people here are conservative. They like to put their money in company stock, or something else that's solid."

"I *know*, Mother. Apparently they don't believe movies are here to stay," said Steve bitterly. "Well, that's your problem. Don't interfere with me when I have a chance to raise the money I need."

"Why don't you just wait an hour or two, and see if it clears up?"

Steve sighed and looked at the handsome clock on the sideboard. His appointment was at three. Ordinarily it would have taken little more than two hours to drive to the city, but today he had planned to allow extra time.

"All right. I'll give it an hour or so," he said. "But I've got to be out of here by noon."

Barbara Wittmer gazed across the table at her son. His features were finer-honed; still, the two looked very much alike. They were also attuned in some mysterious way, so that Steve's repressed fears and worries could induce a stiff neck or migraine headache in Barbara. This morning she had both and, finding no real reason for the tension in the air, blamed it on the weather.

By noon it was raining harder. Steve had passed the time by alternately pacing the house and smoking. Barbara eyed the overflowing ashtray with the special distaste of the reformed smoker and decided she'd had all she could take.

"Well, go on and *go,* if you must," she said. "But promise me you won't drive back after dark. Take a hotel room and drive back tomorrow. You can use my charge card."

"Delighted," said Steve.

He took the card and, when Barbara added a fat little wad of bills, remembered to kiss her on the cheek. Then he picked up his hat and attaché case, shrugged on a raincoat and was out of the front door before Barbara could change her mind.

Steve had a long-standing conviction that people who owned expensive foreign cars were exempt from speed laws. His sleek car seemed in its element on the water-filled road, cutting through the water with a great wake from each wheel, so that a spectator might have been reminded of a hydrofoil. Steve sped down Highway 29 with a glorious disregard for weather conditions or potential road hazards. Consequently, when his eye caught the flashing red lights ten miles out of Mac-Fadden, it was a struggle to stop the sports car.

He hit the brakes hard. Nothing happened. Realizing that they were wet, Steve frantically "burned" them, taking two or three dabs before they became operable. When they did take hold, they sent him into a skid that he barely controlled in time to avoid hitting the patrol car or, possibly, sailing past it into the river. When Steve finally brought his sleek car to a stop, he sat waiting for his pounding heart to settle down.

The patrolman came over and regarded him with disapproval. "Going a little fast there, weren't you?" he asked.

"Yes, Officer, for these conditions, I'm afraid I was. You're absolutely right," Steve said. He looked into the young officer's eyes with disarming frankness, and added in a tone of honest regret, "Slick road, wet brakes . . . I should have been more careful."

"You'd better," the officer agreed. "We've got a bridge out up there. If you hadn't stopped this thing, you'd have been in ten feet of water."

Steve stuck his head out of the window and saw the sullen brown flood moving past. "Who'd have believed it?" he breathed, not without a certain sense of awe at the visible power of the swollen tide.

"Well, I guess you've had your warning," said the patrolman. For a moment youth and enthusiasm broke through his official manner. "Say, that's some car you've got there. Really grabs the road, doesn't she?"

"Sure does." Steve gave him a nice, boyish grin.

"Lucky for you, eh? Well, off you go. Of course, you'll have to turn around and go back to Prairie Chapel. Drive carefully, now."

"I will," Steve promised.

He moved off with great deliberation and, even when the patrolman was out of sight, kept a reasonable speed. His heart was still pounding too hard for comfort. Once he reached a hand to touch the attaché case, lying on the seat beside him. It felt solid and reassuring.

After he came to the turnoff, he was soon on the road to Discovery. Feeling confidence return, he let the speed creep up. He passed a truck, dousing it with water. The truck honked its horn, but Steve's mind was elsewhere.

Before long he met another truck, this one pulling a huge trailer and moving at a good clip. It fairly inundated Steve. For a moment he found himself driving blind, as if he were under a waterfall. The displaced air from the passing vehicle forced his car toward the sodden shoulder. For the second time that day Steve fought for control.

It was all over in a few seconds, but it took much longer, this time, for Steve to regain his calm. He now negotiated the narrow road with extreme caution and at a speed that would allow a near-stop if he were again blinded. In this circumspect manner he finally reached the north–south freeway. Steve breathed a sigh of relief as he shepherded the sports car up the entrance ramp. Now he was home free. He moved into the fast lane, but resolved not to try to break any speed records.

What happened next was like a waking nightmare. Directly ahead he saw a car in the air. He blinked and shook his head; it was still there. It seemed to be floating over the median, and he knew without a shadow of a doubt that it was going to hit him. Steve pumped his brakes frantically, trying to calculate in the instant remaining which, if any, lane might save him from the inevitable impact.

The flyaway car was almost on top of him when he screamed, "God help me!"

Suddenly his car was out of his control, much like the other one, which was now headed in the direction of the guardrail. Steve's car traveled diagonally across the freeway, side by side with the descending car from the other side. Both cars plunged through the guard rail and down the embankment. The other car rolled over and over. Steve's low-centered car stayed on its own four wheels and slid down the steep embankment until it finally came to a stop in the muddy bottom of a ditch.

Steve sat like a stone until he had the presence of mind to start testing himself: head, hands, arms, legs. In mid-examination he thought of the occupants of the other car. He flung open his car door, jumped out and ran. The other car was right side up again, but its top was smashed in. As nearly as Steve could tell, it had had only one occupant, who now appeared to be dead.

Steve stood in the rain and was sick to his stomach until there was nothing left. Then he went back and got into his car and shivered and cried.

When the patrolmen arrived, they were gentle, seeming to understand Steve's extreme agitation. One sat with him and spoke soothingly, not rushing to question him. Finally Steve's story came tumbling out, word by stuttering word.

Shortly thereafter two tow trucks and an ambulance arrived. They took the other accident victim, now proclaimed dead, away and towed away his ruined vehicle. But Steve's car, when pulled out of the mud, showed no more damage than a few scratches and a bent front bumper.

The patrolmen wanted Steve to go to the hospital to be checked over, but he insisted there was no need. "You can see I haven't got a scratch," he assured them.

"We always worry about internal injuries," said the officer.

"Well, if I have an ache or a pain, I'll check in at the hospital," Steve promised.

The patrolman looked at him with concern, noting his pallor and the nervous way he clenched and unclenched his fists.

"You're going to Oklahoma City?" he asked.

"I was. But to tell you the truth, I've kind of . . . lost my appetite for a trip to the city today. I think I'll turn around and drive right back to Prairie Chapel."

"Good decision," said the patrolman, looking immensely cheered. "You're sure you're okay to drive? Had a shock, you know. Well, be careful. One more hour of rain, and we're going to have to close every road in the county."

"I'll be careful," Steve promised, from the heart.

"Good luck!" the patrolman said.

"Thanks." Steve tried to smile. "Thanks a lot. . . ."

He was going to need all the luck anybody would wish him, he thought as he watched the patrol car pull onto the highway and vanish in the misting rain. He sat still for another few minutes, trying to get hold of himself, now that the patrolmen were gone.

He laid his hand on the attaché case, a gesture he had disciplined himself not to make during the time the officers had talked to him, even when one had sat in the car, taking the attaché case by the handle, looking at it before setting it on the floor beside his booted foot. But there had been nothing threatening about those patrolmen, Steve told himself. They had only been helpful and efficient and kind.

In all Steve's life, he had never had to worry about a police officer or a patrolman. Of course, he had played cat-and-mouse games with them on the highway on occasion, but he had always counted on them for just such an emergency as this one. He had taken them for granted, actually, as a sort of necessary nuisance.

To be nervous around a *cop*, to be afraid . . . that was something he had never imagined until now.

Steve shivered and thought perhaps he didn't really have to be scared. Maybe it wasn't too late to turn around.

If only his parents would understand his desperation, and help him. If they wouldn't, who in the world would?

Without thinking, he cried out again for the second time that day, although this time it was a silent cry for help, a prayer. "God, help me."

He turned his car around and started on the long road back.

Chapter Ten

Merry awoke on the morning after the flood, conscious of the most wonderful sense of well-being. Downstairs, she heard occasional voices, unusually muffled; now and then the phone, caught on the first ring. They were letting her sleep.

It would be a shame to waste all this luxury, but she was wide awake, and anticipation made it hard to lie still. Jess would soon be here. He would probably wait until after breakfast, but surely not much longer.

Merry lay back and thought about the preceding day. Even though she had lost her car, she reminded herself, it had been an old one, and only last week the mechanic at Benny's had told her it "needed everything." Maybe the insurance would at least make a down payment on a newer model.

Anyway, the important thing was what had happened

afterward. The flood had enabled Jess and herself to break down the wall that had separated them. She could face her own emotions openly now, and she knew she wanted Jess more than anything else in the world.

Now that Jess had given up on Sally, perhaps he was rediscovering his old feeling for Merry. She wouldn't have even minded being second choice. It would be better than spending the rest of her life as she had been the past six years: always a little restless, a little lonely, as if part of her were missing.

How it had rained! Suddenly Merry's hands went to her unruly hair. She jumped out of bed and headed for the shower, pausing long enough to find and plug in her hot curlers. She seldom subjected her hair to the rigors of electric dryers and steam sets, but this was an emergency.

When she came down to breakfast, her father and mother stared at her.

"Did you remember it's Saturday? No work today," her father reminded her.

"She wouldn't go to work in a sundress, Dan," her mother pointed out. "Where are you going, darling?"

"I hope this is your subtle way of telling me I look nice," Merry said, laughing. "It doesn't speak very well for the way I usually look when I come downstairs."

"You look wonderful," said her father. "You know you'd look fine to us in your old bathrobe. How do you feel this morning?"

"Grand."

"Everyone's been calling," said Mrs. Conner. "Pastor Tucker. The neighbors. David. Sally. And Will, twice already."

"Not Jess?"

"No, not Jess."

"It doesn't matter. He's coming over pretty soon. What's for breakfast?"

After hastily eating a mound of scrambled eggs with toast, she went to see the world from the front window. The sun was out, the sky clearing. Opening the door to test the air, Merry felt a fresh breeze. Sunshine and wind should make short work of the standing water still visible everywhere.

Merry passed the morning calling everyone who had left a number, and was obliged to report on all her misadventures.

Before she could call Will, he had called her again. He'd already had a full report from Libby.

"See, I always told you it was safer to fly," he teased.

"You wouldn't have flown in that."

"You can say that again. I wouldn't even drive in it. Want to do something tonight?"

"Sorry, I already have a date."

"Serves me right. I should have asked you sooner."

Merry hung up the phone thinking what a thoroughly nice guy Will was and looking forward to when Allison would come. She thought Allison's and Will's personalities seemed to complement each other, and she'd be willing to predict that the chemistry would be right.

The afternoon was bright and sunny, but it dragged on for Merry. Could Jess have *forgotten?* She rationalized he had probably assumed she meant this *evening*.

She had spent much of the afternoon reading on the side porch, hoping that Jess would find her there and be reminded of other days. However, it was her father who came looking for her, inviting Merry out to dinner at a newly opened restaurant on the highway. Her safe arrival the night before certainly had provided an occasion for celebration, he explained.

"You and Mom go," Merry said. "I'm expecting Jess any minute."

"Good; I'll call and invite him along," said Dan Conner.

He returned to say that some man had answered Jess's phone; Jess was gone and he didn't know when to expect him.

"That must have been one of the boys Jess sponsors," Merry reasoned. "Probably Jess is on his way here. If he comes soon, we'll join you. But don't wait. Something may have come up."

After her parents left, Merry dropped her pretense of poise and casual acceptance and ran upstairs to check her appearance. The crisp sundress was thoroughly wilted. Her hair, in the warm, damp weather, had lost the curler-induced bounce that had been so becoming. She decided she looked a mess, and, since there seemed no incentive for doing anything about it, she flopped disconsolately on the bed.

She could imagine all kinds of circumstances that could delay Jess, but none that would prevent him from using a telephone. As hour followed long tedious hour, she was led inescapably to one conclusion: it hadn't been that important to Jess, after all.

Hours passed. Her parents must have gone to a movie. It was almost nine o'clock. If she had any pride, she would just get cleaned up again and go somewhere. Libby's perhaps. But Will might be there, and it would be embarrassing to have to explain that she'd been stood up.

When the doorbell rang, Merry ran to the mirror and started in with the comb, then gave it all up as hopeless.

She started downstairs, smothering the impulse to run and fling herself into Jess's arms. Let him explain, first.

Jess presented himself as always, for a date: freshly showered and shaved, perfectly groomed. But he looked pale and tired. Noting this, Merry bit back the sharp comment she had been on the point of flinging at him.

She said, "Come in. I had about given up on you. Is everything all right?"

"Everything's fine. I've just had an exceptionally busy day. Is your mother here?"

"My *mother?*" Merry took a breath, and restored her voice to normal. "My parents went to dinner around six. I thought they'd be home by now. I guess they decided to take in a movie."

"That would make it good and late before they got back, I suppose."

"No, Dad wouldn't go to a very late one. They'll probably be here within the hour. What's the matter, Jess?"

"Nothing's the matter. Actually, I think they'll be pleased. I hope."

"Do you want to sit down?" Merry asked, working hard to control her exasperation. "Or do you want to stand here in the hall and talk about my parents?"

"Let's sit down, of course."

Merry led him through the house to the old glider on the side porch. They sat down. She looked over at Jess and felt his tension pull at her own nerves. He had something on his mind, and it had nothing to do with her. *That* was what hurt. "Can't you tell me what you're agonizing about?" she asked, trying to sound sympathetic instead of annoyed.

Jess thought it over and made a decision. "I can tell

you part of it,'' he said, reaching into his pocket to produce a little drawstring bag. ''I have your mother's jewelry. At least, I think this is all of it. Maybe you can tell me.''

Merry looked stunned. Jess poured the little store into her lap: the heavy gold and cameo brooch, the rings. ''That's it!'' she cried. ''That's all of it.''

''Well, I'm glad to hear it.''

''Jess, where did you get this?''

''That's what I'd hoped you wouldn't ask me. Of course, your parents have the right. They could demand to know, and I'd be obliged to tell them. They would have every right to prosecute, although I hope they don't. The person is sorry and returned the jewelry voluntarily. He's gotten a good insight into what it means to live outside the law. He says he won't try it again, and I believe him.''

''It would be more to the point to find out if his victims believe him. He didn't steal from you.''

''I hope your parents will take my word for it and give him a second chance. All the others involved have agreed to do that.''

''All the others?'' Merry pounced on this statement like a prosecutor. ''Jess MacDonald, do you mean to say that you've been running around all day with your pockets full of stolen property, going into people's houses, telling them this story and expecting them to believe it?''

''Yes. That's exactly what I've been doing.'' Jess's brown eyes examined her face. ''So far, you're the first person who's questioned it.''

''Out loud, that is. Lord knows what they were thinking. Jess, don't you realize you have put yourself in a terrible position? You could be considered an accessory after the fact. If someone *didn't* believe you, they could have you arrested!''

"Do *you* believe me?"

"Of course I believe you. But I've known you most of your life.''

"Well, so has everyone else I had to talk to. Merry, I had a chance to help someone turn his life around. Don't you think that's worth taking a risk?''

Merry wavered. Deep down, she respected Jess's goal, even though his method seemed dangerous. Probably she should simply say so. But another Merry, aggrieved and contrary after a long, disappointing day, kept tugging at her sleeve, prodding her to criticize.

"Obviously, it was important to you to the exclusion of all else," she said. "You let me wait all day."

"I'm sorry. I didn't forget," Jess said. "I thought when you heard what had come up, you'd understand. This person came to me last night, deeply troubled, and we were up most of the night, talking it through. I've been talking to people on his behalf all day. Then I went home and cleaned up, thinking this would be my last stop. If your parents are satisfied, I can finally think about my own personal concerns.''

"I see," said Merry. "Tell me, was there some law against your picking up a phone and calling me?''

"No," Jess admitted. "I should have."

"And *I* should have said yes to Will."

Something in the quality of the silence that followed made Merry wish she hadn't spoken. She looked over at Jess, whose eyes darkened.

"I'm sure it isn't too late," he said quietly.

He rose, tucked the jewelry back in the drawstring bag and put it into Merry's hands.

"If your parents want to discuss this, please have them call me," he said.

Merry's chest felt tight.

"They'll be here any minute," she said. "You might as well stay and talk until they get here."

"There doesn't seem to be a whole lot left to talk about," Jess said, still in that soft, quiet voice.

The front door closed behind him.

It wasn't long after Jess left that Merry's parents arrived. Merry repeated Jess's story without comment and dropped the drawstring bag into her mother's lap.

Mrs. Conner opened it and shrieked with joy. "It's all here. Oh, praise the Lord! Oh, that blessed boy!" She caught a glimpse of Merry's face. "Now mind you, it's not the material value of these things; they would be precious to me if they were brass and glass. *This* came down in the family for three generations, and *this* was given to my grandmother when she was just a young girl!" Her mother said, pointing out particular items to Merry.

"I know, Mom," Merry said patiently. "But don't you think Jess should have told you who took your jewelry?"

"Why, no. I don't even care to know," said Mrs. Conner. "The person returned it; I forgive him, and that's all there is to it."

"We certainly wouldn't want to prosecute someone who voluntarily returned your mother's things," Dan Conner said. "That would be vengeance. Vengeance belongs to the Lord."

"I see."

"What *is* the matter with you, Merry?" her father wanted to know. "You should be happy about this."

"I am, of course. But I seem to be the only one who

170 · TURN, MY BELOVED

has given a second thought to Jess's taking on this responsibility. If someone didn't believe him, it could cause him all sorts of trouble.''

"Who in Prairie Chapel wouldn't believe Jess?'' Mrs. Conner cried.

"I think you're being very technical, Merry,'' Dan Conner said. "I suppose you would have to guard yourself if you lived in a big city, where people don't know each other and one can hardly do a kindness without getting sued. Fortunately, we live more simply here. If Jess can turn somebody around, as he says, without resorting to punishment, why, God bless him is what most folks around here would say. Did you express these sentiments to Jess?''

"Yes.''

"What did he say?''

"Very little. He got super-quiet and soft-spoken, the way he does when he's furious. Then he left. I was mad after being kept waiting all day, but I don't think I said anything *that* offensive.''

"I guess he expected you to be on *his* side,'' Dan Conner said. His mild blue eyes appraised Merry. "Why don't you call Jess and tell him your mother and I are delighted to have her jewelry back? Say that we're eternally grateful. Maybe that will open the way for you two to talk.''

"I think I've done enough talking for one day, Daddy,'' Merry said. She gave them a stiff little smile and kept her eyes wide open, a trick she used to keep from crying. For a moment she looked like a delicately painted china doll. "I'm going up to bed now. Goodnight.''

"It just goes on and on, doesn't it?'' sighed Merry's

mother. "I'd like to shake the both of them, sometimes."

"At the moment your daughter is shaken enough without any help," observed Dan Conner.

At church the next morning, Merry tried to busy herself with her duties. Instead, she found herself an instant celebrity. News of her adventure had traveled all over town. The state paper had obtained pictures of the bridge area, including a stunning shot of Merry's station wagon becalmed in the ebbing floodwaters. Everyone was asking her to repeat her firsthand report.

After the second service, Merry fled to her own office to avoid the coffee crowd in the social hall. She tried to concentrate on some information Friar Tuck had left on her desk regarding seminary offerings, but to no avail.

The noise outside had almost died away when David arrived at the door of her office. "Why are you hiding up here?" he demanded. "Sally and I are whisking you off for lunch."

"Bless you, but I couldn't eat a bite. I had a rotten night. I'm going home to lick my wounds."

"Sally's cooking is just what you need. Merry, I'm really sorry you lost your car."

"That wasn't such a big deal, really. I would have had to do something about it anyway, before I went to seminary—either have it completely overhauled or replace it."

"Still got your heart set on seminary?"

"More all the time. I need to get away, David. I need to start a whole new life."

"Get away from what?" David pulled up a chair and settled down in it, looking over at Merry with concern. "Seminary isn't the Foreign Legion. You don't go there to get away from your problems; you go so you can equip yourself to help others. What's bothering you, Merry? Can you talk about it?''

"I wouldn't mind talking to you, David, but if I talk, I'm going to cry again.''

"Could I take a wild guess? Does it have something to do with Jess?''

Merry nodded.

"Because he loves you and you don't love him?''

"No! No, it's . . . exactly the opposite.''

"Merry, I know I'm no expert in these matters, but Jess gave us a demonstration when he found you were out in the storm that no reasonably intelligent person could misinterpret. I think he loves you very much. Sally thinks so, too.''

Merry raised her head. "Sally! I've thought for a long time that Jess was in love with Sally.''

Sally, arriving at that moment in the doorway, stopped short. "Now that is definitely not true,'' she said.

As David and Merry looked up, startled, Sally marched in and perched on the corner of Merry's desk. Merry found herself confronted by a pair of very earnest dark eyes.

"Where in the world did you get such an idea?'' Sally demanded. "I told you when you came back that Jess and I were *friends*. That's all we've ever been. I had a crush on Jess years ago, but I got over it. I have a healthy ego; I couldn't stay in love with someone so completely *oblivious*.''

Merry gazed into Sally's open face. Sally undoubtedly believed what she was saying. Merry rubbed her forehead in confusion, wondering if she could really have been so mistaken.

"If you care for Jess, Merry, why don't you tell him so?" Sally suggested. "I believe he's been waiting for you all these years. If I were you, I'd marry him as soon as possible. Oh, I know it's none of my business and I shouldn't give advice, but, Merry, don't you realize what you *have* in that man?"

"I don't *have* Jess, Sally," said Merry in a ragged little voice. "If there was a chance, I seem to have blown it. We had a disagreement last night, and apparently I said something unforgivable. I wouldn't have thought so, but Jess went all white and quiet. Then he walked out. He won't be coming back. You think Jess is very saintly, Sally, but I've known him a long time, and he has a stubborn streak a mile wide."

"My goodness!" cried Sally. "Can't you just say you're sorry and start from there?"

"I don't think I said anything to be sorry *for*."

"Well, well. Somebody else has a stubborn streak."

"You don't understand. There's a principle involved. I can't tell you about it; it's Jess's business. But he told me, and I expressed an opinion. I've thought about it, but I haven't changed my mind. So I can't very well say I'm sorry for it, can I? It would be a lie."

"Oh," said David. "No, I don't think you can base a relationship on a lie."

"There's something you could say that would make all that unimportant," Sally argued. "And it *wouldn't* be a lie."

"What is that?"

"Merry, Merry," cried Sally in frustration. "Can't you figure it out for yourself?"

Chapter Eleven

Merry walked the short distance between Sally's apartment building and Jess's with brisk steps that began to slow as she drew nearer. Sally and David had filled her with shrimp creole and confidence; they had heartened her with herb tea and hope. But now she was on her own; for the first time in her life arriving uninvited, unexpected and possibly unwanted.

Of course, Jess must be told of her parents' reaction. Within the bounds of honesty, she could also say she was sorry for inflicting any hurt. If all this failed to open any doors, well . . . she wouldn't think of it right now. She wanted to deliver her message dry-eyed, and in an orderly manner.

Jess's front door stared her in the face. There was nothing to do but ring the bell. The door was opened by Steve Wittmer.

"Come in," said Steve.

"I was looking for Jess," said Merry.

"I hardly thought you came to see me. Jess will be back shortly. In the meantime, come in. I was nerving myself to come and talk to your parents. Maybe I should talk to you instead."

Merry came in, reluctant but curious. She took the chair he offered her. "Why do you want to talk to my parents?" she asked.

"First, I'd like your parents to know that Jess told them the exact and literal truth last night. He had no knowledge of those thefts, nor of the whereabouts of that jewelry, until it was brought to him on Friday night."

"My parents didn't doubt it at all. I came here to thank Jess on their behalf, Steve, and to tell him they don't *want* to know any more about it."

"Really? This doesn't jibe with my observation. Jess came back from his other visits pleased as punch. But when he came home from your house, he looked as if someone had kicked him in the gut."

"He hadn't even talked to my parents. What transpired was . . . between Jess and me."

Steve turned to face her with blazing eyes. "I might have known," he cried. "It would have to be you, the person who can hurt him the most. Don't say anything. Be quiet and *listen*, for once in your life. You want to know how he got the jewelry? He got it from me! How did I get it? I stole it. I'm a thief, do you hear? A lousy, rotten thief!"

Merry stared into Steve's hot dark eyes and, in a rush of insight, saw behind the anger to his humiliation and suffering. She could find nothing in her heart but compassion.

"Oh, Steve, I'm so sorry," she whispered. "You're not, anymore. You gave it back."

Steve was braced for condemnation; the absence very nearly ruined his composure.

"For whatever it's worth, I didn't plan to do it," he finally said, more quietly. "I know it sounds dumb, but it's true. Each time the opportunity magically presented itself, and I walked into it. It's enough to make you believe in the devil. I won't bore you with details, Merry, but I needed fifty thousand dollars in a hurry, for my business. Everywhere I went to raise the money, doors were slammed in my face. I was in a man's house, supposed to be a friend of ours, trying to sell him a five-thousand-dollar share. He laughed at me. Then he went to get me a soft drink, as if I were a little kid. His wife leaves her ring on the piano when she works in the garden; she's done it for years. I saw that thing winking at me, probably worth four times the money I wanted him to invest, and I put it in my pocket. They never even reported it stolen; she thought she lost it, because she's always leaving it around. That's what she told Jess.

"It was always like that, Merry. I never broke in anywhere, or even opened a window. There'd be a party, and I'd see an open jewelry box as I passed the bedroom. I'd take two or three good pieces. Even your house was strictly spur-of-the-moment. I was looking for Jess. He was supposed to come by your house, and I stopped to ask your parents if he had. Nobody was home; the door was standing open. I remembered that heavy gold stuff your mother wears—worth a fortune, these days. I just walked upstairs and got it.

"Even finding out where I could fence the jewelry . . . I simply overheard. It's amazing how hard it is to come by money honestly, but if you decide to be dishonest, the way opens before you."

"That story makes my hair stand on end," said

Merry. "I'm glad you changed your mind. If you really got on that road, it might not be so easy to get off."

"The thought has occurred to me," Steve said. "And then something happened. I had an appointment Friday with a man who uses his business as a front for a more profitable fencing operation. I started driving into the city, and you know what the weather was like. I came within inches of running into the West Fork River. Then a big semi almost ran me off the road. Finally I got on the freeway. Somebody apparently skidded into the wrong lane and got knocked clean over the median. He was headed straight for me, and there wasn't anything I could do to avoid it. I just hollered to God, like a foxhole Christian. I went down the embankment side by side with the other car. Poor guy was killed. His car was totaled, but I didn't get a scratch. I drove my car away. A believer would call it a miracle. I don't know what to call it. If there is a God, why should He do anything for me? I haven't done Him any favors.

"Anyway, the cops came and helped me. I had the jewelry in my attaché case. Every time a man in a uniform came near me, I broke out in a cold sweat. My hands would shake. I didn't realize what a conventional person I am, Merry; I must like being respectable. The upshot was I changed my mind. I came back home and tackled my parents. Laid the whole story on them. Told them how I'd nearly been killed. Told them I'd rather give up my dreams than *feel* the way I felt out there. Guess what they did. Just guess."

Merry, totally immersed in Steve's story, shook her head.

"They threw me out in the rain," Steve announced bitterly. "Dad did, that is. Mother had hysterics. Not for me, mind you. *She* would be disgraced. She wanted to send me to Mexico, have me mail back the jewelry, or lose it, or *anything* to keep her out of it. Dad said I could just hand over the stuff to the police and see if the public defender could get me probation. Or I could hang by my thumbs; he didn't care. 'You take care of yourself, for a change,' he said. He handed me the case and showed me the door.

"When I hit Jess's apartment, I was bawling like a kid. He'd just gotten home. I didn't pay any attention then, but I realize now he was soaking wet and looked dog-tired. But he didn't say a word, not my old buddy."

Steve paused. His eyes had gotten red; he was having trouble controlling his voice. He looked defiantly over at Merry. Her eyes were awash. Seeing this, Steve cleared his throat and was able to continue.

"Jess put his arms around me, and cried with me. He *prayed* for me," he said in a hushed voice. "And after he prayed, he said he thought he'd been given some guidance for me. But first I had to have a hot shower and a change of clothes, and by that time Jess had cooked a hot meal. He took care of me.

"We talked a good part of the night, and Jess came up with this plan. I kicked like a steer. I didn't want Jess to get involved. But he was sure it would work. I finally agreed, after making Jess give me his word that he would tell me if anyone raised a question. If they did, I'd come forward. Jess went to all the people on the Hill first, and after they'd all agreed, he went and talked to my parents. They were surprised and relieved, of course. Said I could come home. Can't say I'm in any hurry. Then Jess got cleaned up and went to your house. I don't think it had occurred to him *you'd* doubt his word."

"I didn't doubt his word for a second," Merry said. "I just didn't think he should risk his reputation, maybe get in trouble with the law himself. It seemed downright foolish, and I said so. Of course, I didn't realize he was shielding *you*."

"I doubt that would have made you any more enthusiastic. However. This doesn't add up, Merry. Jess would understand your feeling that way; it wouldn't have bothered him. But when he came home last night he looked depressed. Kept telling me everything was fine, and then looking heartsick. You must have said something that really cut him down."

"Not that I've been able to remember." Merry mentally rehearsed the conversation again. "I was annoyed with him because I'd waited all day and he never called. I said I might as well have made a date with Will."

"Cheap shot, Merry. I guess you've sensed that Jess is insanely jealous of Will."

"No, I hadn't. I never even considered it. There's no reason. I'm not in love with Will."

"How would Jess know, when you fly off with Will and reappear days later?"

Merry drew herself up. "That requires no explanation, and Jess should know me well enough to know that," she said coolly.

"You know Jess pretty well, don't you? How have *you* been feeling this summer, with Jess at Sally's beck and call, in and out of her apartment any old time? That give you any problem?" Steve's knowing dark eyes held hers, measuring the effect of his words.

There was no place for her to hide. "All right, Steve," Merry said stiffly. "You made your point. Sally says now that Jess was never in love with her. I'm not so sure."

"If you cared about Jess half as much as you care

about Merry and her pride, you'd simply ask him.
Meanwhile, why don't you step into his bedroom and see
whose picture he has on his nightstand.''

''That would be snooping.''

''So snoop, you silly girl. Why it *isn't* Sally's, I can't
imagine. There's a real woman. Beats me why Jess
would set his heart on an arrogant, unforgiving, cold-
natured little minx like you.''

Merry thought that over. ''I'm not cold-natured,'' she
said.

Steve laughed suddenly.

''Maybe not,'' he said. ''You must have something
going besides your looks, or Jess wouldn't want you so
much. Even though he's perfectly capable of loving
worthless people. After all, he still cares for me.''

''Don't say that!'' Merry insisted. *''Nobody's* worthless. God loved us all enough to send His Son to die for
us. I know you don't believe that, but I do.''

''Do you? Doesn't do a whole lot for you, does it?
You sound angelic, but after looking into your face all
these years, I know exactly what *I'm* worth to *you*. Let
me tell you something. I take no stock in religion, but
I'm a compulsive reader. When I'm in a room with
nothing else to read, I browse the Bible. I know all about
that Christlike mind that makes it possible for one to love
the unlovable. Beautiful idea—and I would dismiss it as
so much hot air from watching most of you. Jess is the
only Christian I know who really thinks that way and
lives that way and makes it seem as natural as breathing.
If I ever decide to . . . take a step in that direction, I
hope Jess is around to lead me by the hand.''

Merry had never been so put down. She bowed her
head.

"Of course, if I were a Christian, I wouldn't be allowed to judge you," Steve said. "That's in the Bible, too. You're supposed to know the Bible. Why don't you defend yourself?"

"Because I'm afraid you're right."

Steve leaned back and surveyed her thoughtfully. "I have to tell you something, Merry. You really got to me a few minutes ago. I told you the rotten, selfish thing I'd done and you didn't say a critical word. You gave me the gift of your tears."

"What did you expect?" Merry cried. "Did you really think I was so nasty and self-righteous that I'd be *pleased* to see you in trouble?"

"Why not? Didn't you always imagine I'd come to some bad end?"

"No! I imagined you'd do very well for yourself. You haven't come to a bad end. You turned back. So I think God will help you find a new beginning."

Steve opened his eyes.

"Funny thing you should say that. It's already happening. Jess says, let go and let God. Well, I let go. No credit to me; what choice did I have? I called John Corcoran, one of my partners, just this morning. Told him I couldn't raise the money, and that if he wanted to, he could just buy me out. Jess had already steered me to a corporation lawyer, so I knew pretty well what my contribution was worth. I told him. Maybe it was because of that; maybe he would have done it anyway. But he's working out the financing another way, and I'll be able to make it up as we get into production. What do you think of that?"

Merry said, "I'm not even surprised. You told me Jess prayed for you."

Steve got out a cigarette, then returned it to the pack unlit.

"I ought to go home, I suppose," he said with a sigh. "I can't get a fight out of you. I can get one there without even trying. Or on second thought, maybe not. After all, providing you agree, my parents' position in the community is going to be unsullied."

"I'll never say a word, of course." Merry promised. "How about some coffee before you go?"

"Good idea." He followed Merry to the kitchen. "But if Jess comes before it's made, I'll go. You two need to talk."

"Jess told me last night he didn't think we had anything to talk about," Merry said sadly, measuring coffee and water. While the coffee brewed, she came over to the counter and sat down beside Steve.

"This may be a lost cause," she said. "From the time Jess went back East, we've just had one misunderstanding after another; I don't even know where to begin to start clearing them up. I hope the good Lord gives me the right words."

"When all else fails, try the simple truth," said Steve. "It seems to be working for me."

They drank their coffee in companionable silence. Steve, good as his word, rose to go as soon as he had drained the cup.

"Good luck," he said.

"Good luck to you."

She looked up at him. He looked resolute, but red-eyed. On impulse, she held out her arms. Immediately she was enveloped in a great hug.

"What I really mean is, the Lord be with you," she murmured. The familiar words touched Steve, deep down in his heart. "And also with you," he whispered.

The benediction, coming from Steve, so moved Merry that for some time afterward she sat and dripped tears into her coffee.

Eventually the clutter nagged her away from her meditations. The scattered cups and full ashtray looked out of place on Jess's drainboard. There was sugar spilled on the counter, grounds spilled in the sink. Merry washed and dried the dishes, wiped off the sink and drainboard, then began polishing them with a wad of paper towels.

"I must be dreaming," said Jess from the end of the counter.

Merry jumped. She hadn't heard his key in the lock. Now she was unprepared and tremulous. She held on to the edge of the sink.

"My kitchen didn't pass the white-glove inspection?" Jess suggested.

"Don't be silly. Steve was here when I came, and we had coffee. I was just cleaning up."

"You came to talk to Steve?"

"No. I came to talk to you."

Jess pulled up a stool and sat down, leaned his elbows on the counter and regarded her with polite interest. "I'm listening," he said.

Merry's heart sank. He wasn't going to help her at all.

"Steve insisted on telling me everything," she began. "He was under the erroneous impression that my folks wanted to know more about the robbery. They don't. They're grateful, and I'm supposed to tell you so. That's all. Steve didn't have to tell me anything. Since he did, the secret is safe with me, Jess, and it does make me understand better why you were anxious to shield him. I'm sorry if I . . . overreacted."

Jess shrugged. "No lawyer in the land would disagree with you," he said.

"Well, I'm not your lawyer. So I shouldn't have hassled you about it."

"No problem."

There was an awkward silence.

"Is there something else you think I should know?" Jess prompted.

Merry dropped her eyes. She noticed her hands, gripping the wad of damp paper towels. She looked around.

"Under the sink," Jess said.

Merry opened the sink cupboard and popped the towels into the wastebasket. Then she stole a glance at Jess. He looked remote.

"Sally and David thought I ought to tell you myself," she said hesitantly. "Up until Friday, I didn't think you'd even be interested."

"Is that right?" Jess asked neutrally.

Merry wanted to run and hide, and cry forever. But she had promised herself, this once, to speak the whole truth.

Doggedly she went on. "I don't want to put any sort of burden on you by telling you. Certainly there's nothing you need to do about it."

Jess seemed to have lost color during the conversation, but he spoke calmly, with well-controlled patience. "Merry," he said. "Will you just *tell* me, and get it over with?"

"I love you," Merry whispered in a small voice.

Jess's eyes filled with pain. He hid his face in his hands.

"Jess!" cried Merry, stricken.

Jess took a long breath, and raised his head. "Don't say it if you don't mean it, Merry. Only yesterday you were talking about saying yes to Will."

"I was talking about saying yes to a *date*. I didn't even want *that;* I was just mad. I wanted to be with you. . . ." Merry's control was slipping; her voice trembled. "That's all I ever wanted."

Jess rose in one swift motion and reached for her. Merry ran into his arms. They kissed and clung to each other, laughing and crying. They couldn't get enough of holding each other.

Quite some time elapsed before it occurred to Jess that they couldn't spend the afternoon standing in the tiny kitchen. Gently he guided the dreamy-eyed Merry to his favorite chair in the living room.

"Now that we're reasonably coherent again, let's talk," he said. "Come sit on my lap, where you belong."

"Yes, all right."

"I love you, Merry."

"I love you, Jess."

"Why did it take so long? There's never been anyone for me but you. Even when I was sure I'd lost you, I couldn't seem to get over it. When I saw you in the garden this summer, I was all ready to believe it was meant to be, that you'd come back to me."

"Why didn't you tell me?"

"I started to . . . I can't tell you how many times. Whenever I tried to come close, you seemed to turn away."

"I never meant to. I never will again," she whispered.

"I'll have that in writing, thanks. With witnesses."

"So you shall."

"How soon? And should we have Friar Tuck, or David?"

"Immediately. And both!"

Jess pulled her closer, for the sweet familiar joy of feeling her melt against him.

"Immediately will be almost soon enough," he said, against her lips.